CW00375626

Another Mou

J.C. S

Chris Sledge was born in Leeds, the son of a University Lecturer. He attended Rugby School and was educated at Cambridge University, where he read Economics.

He has spent much of his working life as a management consultant, an occupation which has given him plenty of scope for observing the mistakes which people make in running organisations.

He is married, and lives in North Dorset.

First published in 2009
by Brimstone Press
PO Box 114
Shaftesbury SP7 8XN

www.brimstonepress.co.uk

© J. C. Sledge 2008

Author contact: jcsledge@brimstonepress.co.uk

J. C. Sledge hereby asserts his right to be identified as the author of this work in accordance with section 77 of the Copyright, Designs and Patents Act, 1988

All rights reserved

Designed by Linda Reed and Associates
Shaftesbury SP7 8NE
Email: lindareedassoc@btconnect.com

Cover design by Tam Ying Wah
Cover illustration © istockphoto.com/Ahmad Hamoudah

Printed and bound in Great Britain by
CPI Antony Rowe, Chippenham and Eastbourne

ISBN 978-1-906385-13-2

Another Mouth has Passed

J. C. Sledge

Brimstone Press

1

'Morning, Edward. Leg any better?'

Edward looked for a moment as though he was surprised to be asked. Then, grasping his stick, he replied: 'No, Paul. But thanks for asking.'

The two men had met outside the village Post Office in Horton Fence. On cold days people tended just to nod at each other before they went in to buy their postage stamps or what little else was available for sale. Today, however, being mild and quite sunny, there was more of an incentive to stay and chat.

'I gather the Parish Council is quite warm to the idea of the social housing development,' Paul said, in his usual neutral fashion.

'Puh!' Edward snorted. 'They would be.'

'I think they were just being sounded out informally,' Paul remarked. 'No plans have been put in yet.'

'I haven't really been following it,' Edward said. 'Edith mentioned it a while back, and I was hoping it would just go away and die. But in view of what you say I'd better start taking an interest.' He used his stick to begin propelling himself forward, saying: 'Can you spare a minute to show me where they're thinking of putting it?'

'Of course.'

Paul Preece was the acknowledged source of information on anything to do with local history and plans even though, as far as Edward was aware, he wasn't a member of any of the official bodies.

'Can't see that Horton Fence is the right sort of place for social housing,' Edward said. 'If they need some they'd do better to put it in Crapwell. It's on the main road. The trains stop there. Twenty minutes in to Exeter by train. Ideal for people who can't afford cars.'

It was pointless expecting inhabitants of Horton Fence, especially the male ones, to call the town by its correct name. Even most of the wives had given up trying. And it was true that Clapwell was a featureless sort of place, full of industrial estates and not a great deal else. The previous year an Indian curry house had been opened in the town centre, thereby fixing the town's name for ever in the minds of Edward and many others.

The best thing that can be said for Crapwell, Edward thought as he struggled to keep up with Paul, who was much slimmer and fitter, is that it's seven miles away. On the far side of the hill, which provides a good barrier against traffic noise. Horton Fence is a different world. Not much through traffic. Plenty of pleasant houses. The modern ones aren't brilliant, but they aren't ostentatious either. And that marvellous view to the south, particularly for people like me who are smart enough to live at the top part of the village. On a clear day you can see right down to the water.

'It's the Church Field site, as I'm sure you know,' Paul said, stopping by the wall which shielded the area from view.

'I feared that's what you were going to tell me. Right slap in the middle of the village, eh?'

'Sooner or later something was bound to be built here,' Paul said.

The way you're talking, I'm beginning to think you like the idea, Edward thought, surveying his colleague. I'm not taken in by your careful Civil Service way of speaking. Paul Preece. A sort of ironed out flat kind of name. A sort of ironed out flat kind of person, come to that. Not an inch of spare flesh on him. Kept all his hair, too. Galling thing is, I believe he's at least 67 if not older. And I don't get my pension until next year.

Edward kept his thoughts to himself, then distracted himself from them by asking: 'Mind if I have a pipe?'

'Of course not. Nice to see someone keeping the habit going.'

Edward nodded as he fiddled about with the tobacco, using the end of his match. Let me not think uncharitable thoughts.

'My father was a pipe smoker,' Paul said. 'I've always rather liked the smell.'

'I feel like a pariah in my own house when I light up,' Edward said, not trying to keep the irritation out of his voice. 'Especially when my daughters are around. The way they go on, you'd think Baby'd keel over and die the moment it sees a pipe.'

Paul chuckled, thinking of the censures he had received from his own son and daughter over the years and then said, gesturing at the field: 'Well, this is it.'

'And how many houses are they thinking of putting here?' Edward asked, suspiciously.

'Can't say. We'd have to wait for the plans. If anyone puts any in.'

'Whose land is it now? Do you know?'

Paul thought for a minute, as if he was wondering whether it was wise to reveal what he knew.

'As I understand it,' he said, choosing his words with care, 'it still belongs to the Church but they're willing to let it go if the Council will give them some more land so they can extend the cemetery a bit.'

'Weren't they supposed to be putting a Parish Hall on it?'

'Oh, yes, all that saga about the Cuthbertson bequest. I think things have moved on a bit since then.'

'Ah.'

'As you'll know, the field used to belong to the Old Rectory.' Paul jerked his thumb in the direction of the large grey building on the far side of the field. 'When Lady

Cuthbertson died she left the house to her nephew with a stipulation that he should give the field to the Church so that they could build a Parish Hall. The nephew didn't like the idea and spent lots of money with lawyers trying to prove that his aunt was mentally incapable when she signed her will. Then when he found that he couldn't get title to the house unless he did what his aunt had said he tried to put in a provision of his own saying that he didn't have to hand it over for twenty years, because she hadn't specified a time in the will.'

'Makes you wonder why she didn't just leave the land directly to the Church, doesn't it?'

'That would have made things easier, certainly. I expect she wanted to demonstrate her family's continuing commitment to the Church. Anyway, eventually he had to hand it over, which he did with very bad grace. Then the Church couldn't make up its mind what kind of a building it wanted.'

'And whatever ideas they came up with, either the Vicar blocked it or old Farquharson objected.'

'Yes. Both, as I understand it. Then we got combined with the parish at Motherston and they thought it might be a better idea to locate it there as Motherston's bigger. And now they say they can't afford it and they're not sure it's needed anyway.'

'There's your good old Parochial Church Council for you. Decision making ability of a bunch of sheep.' Edward took another puff on his pipe and then said: 'Sorry, that was unkind. I know Dorothy works very hard for the PCC.'

'She certainly does,' Paul replied, not sounding as though he had taken offence. 'Though I have to agree with you. Anyway, in the end, the Church decided that the best way to honour the spirit of Lady Cuthbertson's will was to make the land available for some purpose which was of benefit to the community.'

'Oh, great. So the community will benefit by having all manner of rags, tags and bobtails dumped in the middle of the village.'

'It hasn't happened yet, Edward. Nobody says it will.'

'Put it at Crapwell, I say. Anyway, thanks for letting me know, Paul. I must get back so I can supervise Byron.'

'Byron?' For the first time Paul showed genuine surprise in his voice.

'Yes, ridiculous name, isn't it. The big goofy lad who does my garden twice a week. Unless you go and see what he's doing every half hour either he's fallen asleep or he's deserted the task you've given him and invented a different one of his own. He's my responsibility today because Edith's been summoned to do yet another day's Kiddywatch.'

Edward turned and set off purposefully up the street. Paul observed that he seemed able to walk without any obvious difficulty. Perhaps the stick, with its large and menacing knob, was more a statement of attitude than a necessary walking aid.

'If this social housing thing does happen I can't see our friend Mr Jackson-Wright liking it,' Paul said, finishing his lunchtime salad.

'Poor old Edward,' Dorothy replied. 'I expect his leg problem makes him grumpy.'

'From the way he was going on this morning I would say most things do.'

'They give very generous drinks parties. And Edith's a sweetie.'

'Yes, she is. Anyway, nothing may come of it'.

'It's a lovely day. I must try and get some gardening done later. Have you got time to cut some of that ivy down?

'Yes, some time, I expect. I've said I'd go and see someone in Motherston this afternoon. He's got some old baptism records I want to have a look at.'

‘And you have to do that today? It may rain again tomorrow.’

‘I don’t want to disappoint the old boy. He sounded so pleased with himself that he’d found them for me.’

Dorothy collected the plates and took them into the kitchen, trying not to notice the familiar grey feeling which spent so much of its time these days settling on her. When they had first moved to Horton Fence, shortly after Paul had retired from the Home Office, they spent virtually all their time together. First there was the house to alter and redecorate, and when they weren’t doing that they made a point of going on long walks. Paul had bought them a booklet of 40 pub walks; by the end of their second summer Dorothy worked out that they had done over 30 of them. Five years later the others were still to do. When she tried to get Paul interested again all she got were brush-offs along the lines of ‘Who wants to have lunch at the Crapwell Arms?’

I suppose it’s all my fault, she thought, sighing and hoping she hadn’t said the words out loud. She knew she was prone to do so these days. Paul was quite sharp with her when he heard her, telling her it was an old woman’s habit and she wasn’t an old woman yet. It was her idea that they should join the local History Society, and within a few months Paul had become so absorbed in the subject that it seemed to have taken over his life. Of course it was a good thing for him to take up a new interest in retirement, but surely not to the extent of making her feel so excluded? Doesn’t surprise me, her daughter Harriet had said, I’ve always said he was a frustrated academic.

And now Harriet had decamped to Australia with her husband. Getting DVDs of her grandchildren was a pleasure, but they only made her feel how strongly she wanted to be with them, to pick them up and cuddle them… And as for Malcolm; no, she told herself, I don’t feel strong enough to think about Malcolm today.

She went to collect the remaining plates from lunch, to find Paul still puzzling about his conversation with Edward Jackson-Wright.

'I can't understand the man,' he said. 'He's obviously intelligent, but I can't work out what he does all day. Except read the Telegraph. He doesn't seem to do anything in the village.'

'Oh, that's not fair. He often helps out with the bar and things at the Village Hall.'

'Only because Edith pushes him into it.'

'And they spend a lot of time with their grandchildren,' Dorothy said, trying not to feel jealous.

'Do they? I know she does. And he can't do much in the garden. Or play golf, with his leg in that state. Sad, really. Or am I being unfair?'

'You're beginning to sound like the Pharisee who gave thanks to God because he wasn't as other men were,' Dorothy replied, not caring if she sounded waspish.

Paul smiled to himself, accepting the rebuke.

'Ah, well,' he said. 'Must be off. Back by tea-time, I hope.'

Byron went across to conceal himself behind the hedge, checked that nobody could see him and then unzipped his trousers. He knew that he was welcome to use the Jackson-Wrights' downstairs toilet, but he preferred not to trouble them. And he was fairly certain that he had seen Mr Jackson-Wright himself having a discreet leak outside on occasion.

Problem was, particularly when he had a pee out of doors, his cock tended to have other ideas when he fingered it, trying to get all the wet off before he put it away. Here we go again, he thought, feeling it swell up uncomfortably inside his pants. And every time I'm here and it happens I think of that day last summer when Mr Jackson-Wright's daughter was here. Lovely long legs, a peaches and cream complexion, long blonde hair and what a figure! She was stretched out on the lower lawn in her bikini. Baby was in its pram, asleep. She can't have realised I was working here, because when I came round the corner carrying a sack of cuttings she was obviously startled. The top half of her bikini was covering her breasts, but I could see it was only lying on them, she'd undone the strap. Her hand was on the lower half but I'll swear it was inside when I first caught sight of her.

'Hi,' she said, trying to sound all casual. 'Bit hot for that, isn't it?'

Bit hot for what you're doing, lady.

Byron stumped off angrily towards the bottom of the garden, telling his cock to subside and knowing perfectly well that it wasn't about to do so.

The Jackson-Wrights were giving one of their drinks parties. As usual, they had succeeded in picking a fine day, so their guests were free to wander through the house, go outside and admire Edith's garden, sit by the pond, admire the view – and generally remind themselves, if they felt so inclined, that there was no shortage of money as well as generosity being displayed. Edward had long since given up charging around himself filling up his guests' glasses, and probably not just because of his lameness. Today the task was being carried out by three young waiters in immaculate white shirts and bow ties.

'Edward tells me there's going to be some ghastly social housing development at Church Field.' Charles Crawford had only heard this a couple of minutes previously.

'Oh, no, surely not!'

'Whose idea was that?' Charles's wife, and Mrs Henshaw, sounded even more affronted than he did.

'God only knows.'

'John Prescott, I expect,' Mrs Henshaw said. 'He sees it as his mission to cover the entire bloody country with mean little houses. For mean little people.'

'They can't force it on us, surely?'

Paul Preece was on hand to supply a few much needed facts.

'They'd have to get planning permission. So if we don't like what's proposed, we have our chance to say so.'

'A fat lot of comfort that'll be.' Mrs Henshaw had been preoccupied mainly with getting her wine glass refilled, but was now ready to join in the debate with vigour. All Mrs Henshaw's opinions were expressed with vigour, even when she didn't have a wine glass in her hand. 'The Council puts forward the idea, and the Council has the power to decide whether it should be approved. We don't really have a say at all. Sham democracy, that's what it is.'

'I think you'll find it isn't the Council,' Paul observed.

'What are you talking about?' Mrs Henshaw rounded on him. 'The Council's the planning authority.'

'Yes, I know that. What I meant is that it wouldn't be the Council which puts forward any plans. The Council doesn't provide social housing any more. It would have to appoint a Housing Association.'

'What's a Housing Association?' Mrs Henshaw was clearly prepared to damn it, whatever it was.

'It's a...successor body to a Council,' Paul replied, deciding to keep matters simple although he knew this wouldn't get many marks as an official definition. 'It gets Government money to help it build houses for people who need them and can't afford their own. Government doesn't want Councils to be direct providers any more.'

'Same thing, different name, is that what you're saying?'

'I don't think they'd see it that way.' Paul observed drily, beginning to wish he hadn't offered to help.

'And who will they decide to put here?'

'They don't decide. That's not their responsibility. They're just the landlord.'

This provoked Charles Crawford to rejoin the battle.

'You mean this outfit puts up the houses on Government money and hasn't got a clue who's going to live in them?'

'Let me explain,' Paul said, sensing that the bull was in danger of being grasped firmly by the tail and that there were plenty of volunteers ready to do the grasping. 'The District Council has the legal responsibility for maintaining the register of people in housing need. If it doesn't provide housing itself any longer, as ours doesn't, it appoints a Housing Association to build them and manage them. And the Council determines who's going to live in them.'

'So how do they know what type of houses to build?'

Give me patience.

'They talk to each other. They're allowed to do that, you know.'

Charles Crawford smiled, acknowledging the point.

'I'm glad you're up to speed with these things, Paul. We can do no end of damage to our blood pressure if we don't understand the system.'

'Well, whatever the system is, I don't like it,' Mrs Henshaw said, looking around in the hope of catching the waiter's eye. 'Horton Fence is fine as it is. That's why we all enjoy living here. I can see no merit in bringing any change to the village.'

'Let's see what Frank has to say,' Barbara Crawford suggested, seeing him walking in their direction and not wanting to lose the chance of involving him. Frank was a regular at everyone's parties as he seemed incurably genial and – being an electrician – most people in the village had reason to be grateful to him for rescuing them from actual or potential disasters of one sort and another. As he had lived in the village for all his working life – and done his stint on the Parish Council – he was held in respect by more or less everyone. A good man for drinks parties, even though no-one could ever remember him giving one himself, but not a candidate for dinner parties.

'We're trying to make sense of this social housing proposal,' Barbara said.

'Why're you bothering your heads about it?' Frank replied, smiling at them indulgently. 'It's miles away. If it ever happens.'

'But it might.'

'So where's the harm in that?'

'Well...' Charles began, then realised it might be wiser to play for time.

'Look,' Frank said. 'My son went into the same trade as me. If he wanted to come back and live here, how could he afford to buy a house?'

'Is that what he's thinking of doing?'

'That's not the point,' Frank said. 'I'm sure you take my meaning.'

With which, Frank moved on. Mrs Henshaw did likewise, having failed to locate a wine waiter.

The Crawfords also made their way towards a different part of the garden, but paused when they saw that a small boy was in danger of cannoning into their legs.

'Toby, come here,' his mother commanded. 'You're being a pest again.' She bent down to pick him up. Charles found it impossible not to observe the amount of cleavage she was displaying, and saw no good reason why he should look elsewhere.

'Hi,' she said, smiling and pushing her blonde hair back with her spare hand. 'I'm Sandra. Are Mum and Dad looking after you properly?'

'They always do. Best parties in the village.'

'You've got some other children as well, haven't you?' Barbara enquired.

Sandra looked puzzled. 'No, afraid not. This one's more than enough for me.'

'Oh.'

Sandra suddenly realised how the confusion had arisen.

'Maybe you're thinking about my sister Caroline. She has three of them. Not here today. They've all got runny noses. Or runny other bits we'd rather not talk about.'

'Ah, yes, that must be it,' Barbara said, glad to be rescued from her embarrassment. 'I think you and she look rather similar?'

'Yes, we do,' Sandra replied, cheerfully. 'People are always mistaking us for each other. Not that either of us minds that much.'

'Another lovely blonde lady, then?' Charles said. This beats having to consider the prospect of social housing in the village.

'Funny, isn't it. There's Caroline and me who are the blondes, then it changed. Laura's number three, she's still at Uni. She's quite dark.' And serious. And intense. Not like the rest of us at all. 'Then there's little Ellie, who came along long after Mum and Dad thought they'd finished. She's got the most gorgeous wavy gold hair. Envy, envy!' And freckles. And lovely mischievous green eyes. Like Mummy's, only better. And we all love her to bits.

Toby made a determined effort to break free from his mother's grasp.

'Excuse us,' Sandra said, letting him down but insisting on clamping his hand inside hers. 'The little master wishes to move on.'

She avoided getting caught up in conversation with any of the other guests and took Toby to sit by the edge of the pond, encouraging him to try to spot the goldfish.

After a minute or so she became aware that someone else had come across to the pond, and she heard a very pleasant and relaxed voice asking: 'How many have you counted, then?'

Sandra looked up, making sure that she was still firmly hanging on to Toby. The question had come from a tall, youngish man with blue eyes, slightly reddish hair, and a manner every bit as agreeable as his voice.

'Hello,' she said, a little self-consciously. 'I don't think we've met. I'm Sandra. I'm the daughter of the house. Or one of them, I should say.'

'Mike Tayfield. Pleased to meet you.'

'You're local?'

'Since six months ago, yes. And yourself?'

'Afraid not. Weekend visitor. Back to the smoke this afternoon.'

'I met your parents at a cheese and wine do a few weeks ago. It's very kind of them to invite us.'

Sensing that Toby was getting bored with looking at the pond Sandra hoisted him on to her shoulder and stood up. She still found herself looking up at Mike.

'They're very hospitable,' she said. 'They like making newcomers to the village feel welcome. I assume you live in the village?'

'Right in the centre.'

'Oh. So you'd be close to this social housing thing they're all talking about?'

'If it happens,' Mike said, smiling.

'Did you know about it when you bought your house?'

'It showed up as a possibility when the search was done.'

'But that didn't worry you?'

'Well, put it this way. On a teacher's salary there aren't many houses in a village of this type which are in my price range.'

'Ah,' Sandra said, concerned that she might have put her foot in it. Or both feet, possibly. 'Where do you teach?' she asked, hurriedly.

'Clapwell. If I'm still allowed to call it that.'

'Not many do,' Sandra replied, beginning to regain her composure.

'Anyway,' Mike said, seeing that Toby was getting restless again, 'it was nice to meet you. But I'd better go and find where my wife's got to.'

Sandra smiled, rebuking herself for feeling disappointed to discover that he had a wife. She watched him make his way across the lawn – all long legs and easy charm – but lost him from sight before she could identify her.

The standard of thirty-somethings in Horton Fence is definitely improving, she told herself. He's in a different league from Caroline's stodgy husband, that's for sure.

2

'What about Horton Fence. Is it worth putting on the list?'

The senior members of the Housing Association's Development Department were meeting to produce the first draft of their bid request for future funding.

'That's one of the tricky ones,' Howard observed. 'I'm not at all sure the District Council has got its ducks in a row.'

As Director of Development Howard had the casting vote. But, being keen not to stamp on the enthusiasm of one of his subordinates, he was willing to engage in a debate.

'What's concerning you?'

'They've been talking about wanting to put young families there. I don't think that's Horton Fence, somehow. The place is full of the affluent retired.'

'Pushing up house prices and making it somewhere near impossible for locals to get on the property ladder.'

'Which is a fair argument. But it doesn't dislodge me from my view.'

'So what would you prefer to see there?'

'Something for older people, perhaps. The need there must be just as strong. And it would be more likely to gain acceptance, locally.'

'Would they buy?'

'Difficult to say.'

'Because it won't stack up unless we do mixed tenure. And the District Council's really into shared ownership.'

'Do we know what the land will cost?'

'Not exactly. The Council's talking about some complicated land swap deal with the Church. And the local Church can't take a decision, it has to go to the Diocese.'

Howard threw his hands into the air, and then said: 'There must be some easier projects we can put in?'

'We don't want to lose the relationship with the District Council. They want to work with us on this one.'

'OK. Fair point. Put it in if they're that keen on it. If it fails, it fails. Crocodile tears at dawn, and all that. What's next?'

'Do come in, dear,' Barbara said, using her most unctuous tone of voice to cover her uncertainty. 'I think it's dreadful of me that you've been our neighbours for, what, nearly two years now and this is the first time we've invited you in.'

'Not a problem,' Valerie replied. Which she knew was entirely true, though she wondered if she had said so with a bit too much emphasis.

'I'll just get the coffee.'

Valerie looked round the drawing room. Pencil sketches of dogs, pictures of huntsmen jumping across hedges. One or two rather watery paintings of somewhere by the coast, probably in Italy. She wondered, with slight alarm, whether a large Labrador was about to be let loose on her as soon as the door was re-opened.

Barbara reappeared with the coffee. Before she closed the drawing room door behind her Valerie could hear the sounds of a dog expressing its disgruntlement about being excluded.

'Far too bouncy, he is. He's not allowed in here until late at night when there's just Charles and me here. Then all he's good for is curling up in front of the fire.'

Valerie smiled, and then said: 'It's remarkable what a difference it makes to the view from one house higher up.'

'Yes, dear, you're right. It doesn't quite match the view from Edward and Edith's, but we're not far off.'

'We haven't been there,' Valerie replied, cancelling her smile. If you call me dear again I'm going to make this a very short visit.

'You must get a very different view over the village,' Barbara said. 'Your house is all sort of hidden away from us.'

'It gives us a long back garden,' Valerie commented.

'I hope our trees down there don't annoy you.' Barbara waved her arm in the general direction of Valerie's house.

'Not at all. The view's to the south, isn't it?'

'If there is anything we're doing here which bothers you, you must let us know. Dear old Mrs Walsh seemed to spend all her time indoors so I'm afraid we got into the way of thinking that there really wasn't anybody next door. Charles used to call her the dormouse, you know.'

What a nice man he must be. But if he was one too it would take rather a large teapot to contain him.

'We're quite happy with things as they are.'

'Good. And you've settled in all right?'

'Yes, we enjoy it here.'

'I'm pleased to hear it. I do wonder sometimes, we never seem to see you at events in the village.'

'You can blame it on work, I suppose.'

'So your husband has to work long hours?'

'All GPs do, these days. And when he's away from work he likes to get right away.'

'So that people don't tell him about their aches and pains on social occasions?'

'Exactly,' Valerie replied, reinstituting the smile. 'That's why he's taken up fishing.'

'And you work also?'

'I'm the lucky one. I can work from home.'

'As...?'

'I'm an illustrator. I hide away in an upstairs room and live in my own world.'

'And you clearly love doing it. What kind of work do you do?'

Ah, good. For a moment I thought she was going to ask me if I did doggy portraits.

'I trained as a botanical illustrator. But there isn't a great deal of that kind of work about. At the moment I'm doing some work for a friend who writes children's books.'

'And you have a child of your own, yes?'

'Heather. Yes. She takes after me, I think. Another solitary. Comes home from school and she's quite happy on her own. Writing stories is her thing this year.'

'Are they any good?'

Valerie paused. 'Probably not. But I'm her mother, and I'm proud of her.'

'We're like that, aren't we?' Barbara's tone softened. 'Even when they're miles away.'

'Which is where yours are, I take it?'

'One followed his father into the army, and he'll be somewhere in Germany for another year or more. Our younger boy does something I've never quite understood in the City, makes pots of money, but doesn't often get to see us.'

'You sound as though you miss them.'

'One does. Though I don't exactly miss their wives.'

Perhaps I *can* take to her, Valerie thought. But maybe it wouldn't feel right to ask her to say any more.

'I suppose you've heard about this social housing thing?' Mrs Crawford said, aware of the silence.

Valerie looked blank.

'I take that as a no,' Barbara said, smiling a bit ruefully.

'Quite right,' Valerie said, hoping she wasn't causing offence.

'There's a proposal to use the Church Field site to put up houses for all sorts of strange people to rent. Some of us are rather concerned about it.'

'Is it going to happen? Or is it just an idea?'

'I hope it's an idea which will go away.'

'Is it bound to be a bad thing?'

'Well, what do you think?' Barbara said, suddenly sounding rather aggressive.

'It's the first I've heard about it. I'm not sure I know enough to have a view.'

'Possibly not,' Barbara said, relenting. 'But I'm worried about the sort of people it might bring into the village. Do you see what I'm getting at?'

Valerie hesitated, and then asked: 'Do we know anything about...who'd be living in the houses?'

'Not yet. But they'd be people who can't afford to buy their own property. I think that says something about the kind of people we might be in for.'

Valerie paused before she replied, wondering whether it was worth taking the risk of antagonising her neighbour needlessly.

'Well, all I can say is this. When people who are registered with the practice ask for an appointment at Simon's surgery he sees them. Whoever they are.'

'Yes, fair comment. Though it's not exactly a...parallel. A bit more coffee?'

'No, I'm fine, thanks. And I must be away in a minute.'

'Well, let's hope that those of us who are getting worried about it are becoming all worked up about nothing. But there is one other thing I wanted to mention to you. Would you be willing to give us a hand with the Church Fete this summer?'

'We're not churchgoers, Mrs Crawford.'

'Barbara, please.'

Valerie smiled.

'It's a fund raiser,' Barbara explained. 'And one of our main village events. If new people are able to help it stops the thing getting stale. And it's a fun day.'

'What did you have in mind, Barbara?'

'I don't know, exactly. But those of us who take on the job of running the event are always looking for more people to help. Some of the old stagers are falling by the wayside.'

'Well, let me know nearer the time. I'm not sure about running a stall, but I'm sure we can let you have a few things to sell. We do want to do our bit, you know.'

'That's good of you.'

'On which note,' Valerie said. 'It's time I left you in peace. Thank you for inviting me.'

A couple of days later Barbara picked up an envelope which had arrived on her doormat, clearly hand delivered. The message inside the card said:

Dear Barbara

Thank you so much for inviting me for coffee on Wednesday. I'm not a natural socialiser, as you probably gathered, so I really appreciated your taking the time with me.

I'll see what I can do to contribute to your Fete but I think I should let you know that yesterday my mother rang to say that, as I had been fearing, my father has terminal cancer. As I have no brothers or sisters you'll understand that my time is going to be rather taken up with family matters.

With best wishes

Valerie Burlington.

When Charles read the card he commented, with genuine sympathy: 'Poor lady, it's going to be difficult for her. What's she like?'

'Dark and serious. And very private.' And no cleavage for you to get interested in.

Dorothy Preece sighed as she lugged the vacuum cleaner past the back of the pews in the nave and began to deal with the second main aisle. This is going to take ages, she thought – then realised she had spoken the words aloud. I must get out of this habit, she told herself; and not just because it annoys Paul and he gets quite sharp with me. He's right, it is an old woman's habit. And I don't want to turn into an old woman who only has herself to talk to.

I might get on faster if this wretched machine wasn't so inefficient. And heavy. Next time I really will have to bring our own. If I can face the thought of getting it in and out of the car and up the steps. And it would be a bit pleasanter if I could still share the task with someone else. Three years ago there seemed to be plenty of people willing to do the cleaning, now we seem to be struggling to get one volunteer a month, let alone the two it needs. Betty Henshaw gave up because she said her doctor had told her not to move anything heavy because of her back. I'm not sure that's the real reason. A couple have left the village, and their houses have been bought by weekenders. It's getting more and more of a struggle to keep things going in the parish.

Dorothy stood up, aware that she was allowing herself to get into a downward spiral of gloomy thoughts, and aware also that her back was getting tired. The church seemed dull; it was a cloudy day, and the building needed sunshine to bring it to life when it was empty of people. But what people? In the seven years she and Paul had lived in the village the congregation had progressively declined; a club for the over 60's, Paul had called it, and they'll not be going on for that much longer. Why wear yourself out trying to keep it going, he had asked her. You can't agree among yourselves what kind of services you want, the Vicar seems more interested in what's going on at Motherston because it's a bigger place and there are more children who come to church there.

I just wish he wouldn't be so rational about everything, she thought, resuming her task. It's difficult to argue against what he says, because a part of me knows he's right. And everybody says it would be a shame if the church couldn't keep going, even those who never come to a church service. But what do they do to keep it going? Give it just enough money to stop it falling down, I suppose. And perhaps put in an appearance at the Fete and one or two other events. But precious little else.

But where would we stand if the Church Field site does get sold for this housing development I keep hearing about? For a moment Dorothy's thoughts brightened; that could solve a lot of our financial problems, we'd be able to get away from the endless grind of small scale fund-raising efforts. Then she realised that the Diocese would take the decision about whether to sell, and the Diocese would determine what happened to the proceeds. So no comfort there, or at least no guarantee of comfort.

She bent down to collect a couple of pieces of paper which were lying on the floor; one was a child's drawing, the other appeared to be a note which an adult had dropped. She wondered whether she was being intrusive in unfolding it, but told herself that it might be something important and that she might be thanked for retrieving it. The note merely said Anne, and gave a home number and a mobile number. She didn't recognise the writing, but she decided to hang on to the note, just in case it mattered to someone. After all, a note with a lady's phone number wasn't the kind of thing you expect to find dropped on the floor of a church. She smiled at the thought of producing it at an unexpected moment and testing the reaction. Charles Crawford, perhaps? At least he was a churchgoer, though not as regular in his attendance as Barbara. And his interest in women was clear to everybody.

Dorothy's spirits lifted, and completing the remainder of the aisle only took her a few more minutes. Just the carpet in the chancel and that'll have to be it, though I'll have to unplug the machine and get down on my hands and knees to find the socket by the base of the organ. The first time I did the cleaning there I almost knocked myself out, banging the back of my head against the carved figure at the end of the choir stall when I got up. I had a headache for days after that experience.

And it wasn't much easier this time. The machine cut out twice in the first couple of minutes; after the second incident Dorothy got down on her knees and discovered that the socket itself was loose. As soon as she took the vacuum cleaner towards the end of its range the cord started to cause the problem by pulling everything away from the wall. For a moment Dorothy looked round, somehow imagining that there would be a small screwdriver sitting conveniently on one of the choir stalls; then she laughed at her silliness, but all her cheerfulness of a minute ago had evaporated. That's what the church has come to, she thought. Tired and tatty, with just about everything needing an overhaul. This is a sad chore. Going to church used to be a joy. Where's the joy now? Or is it me? Am I being tested, and found wanting? Maybe that's it. God tests your faith; He wants to know whether you're worthy of Him, and of what He did for you. That's right. I must try harder. What sort of a believer am I if I'm going to allow myself to get defeated by something as trivial as a loose connection?

Well, she thought, let's recognise the inevitable. I can't get to the top end of the chancel, so I'd better unplug the thing before I do any more damage. Perhaps I can come back this afternoon and screw everything back into place. She bent down once more, trying carefully to take the plug at the end of the cord out of the socket without worsening things – and worrying about whether she was causing a safety problem which might get worse. I need to talk to Mavis about this; she's still one of the Church Wardens, even though she's often not well enough to come to services. Or maybe I should talk to her husband, to save her the worry. Only he's so abrupt on the phone, if I get him I always feel guilty about ringing...

'Excuse me...'

Dorothy hadn't heard the church door being opened, but as soon as she heard a voice she became aware that her back end was sticking out from next to the choir stalls. She scrambled to her feet, hoping she didn't appear as undignified as she felt.

'I'm sorry...'

'I hadn't heard you come in,' Dorothy said, advancing towards the couple standing just inside the door.

'We didn't mean to disturb you.' The voice was male, and sounded distinctly antipodean.

'Oh, I'm just tidying up. Nothing important.' Dorothy pushed a loose strand of grey hair back from her forehead, aware of how messy she must look. The couple in front of her were at least thirty years younger than her.

'It's my husband's first visit here.' Her voice was much more English. 'I wanted to show him the village where I was born.'

'Ah,' Dorothy said. 'How interesting. Which was your parents' house?' Then she blushed, realising that they might still be living here and she might know them.

'They lived down at the lower end of the village. We moved away when I was five, but I still have a vague picture in my mind of how things were.'

'And how do you find it now?' Dorothy enquired, hoping she wasn't sounding too apprehensive.

'It's all just great,' the husband replied. 'I'm Shane Graham,' he announced, thrusting his hand in Dorothy's direction.

Dorothy accepted the handshake, wincing both because of its firmness and because of the name of its owner. How can any parent saddle their son with a name as ugly as Shane?

'I just can't get used to how old everything is here,' Shane said. 'I come from Auckland. Old for us is 1890. Really old's 1840. I mean, how long has this church been here?'

'We know there's been a church here since about 1170. Much of what you see is from later on, but the building's always been here.'

'Come on,' the wife said, 'let's walk round. We're getting in the way.'

'Not at all,' Dorothy said, but she was relieved to be able to go back to collect her various items of cleaning equipment.

A few minutes later she was ready to leave, and made her way towards the door.

'Is it all right if we stay and look round a bit longer?' Shane asked. 'There's just so much history and atmosphere here, I can't get enough of it.'

'Of course,' Dorothy said, beginning to warm to him because of his enthusiasm. 'It's nice to know our church is appreciated.'

'It certainly is.'

As Dorothy made her way towards the back of the church to return the vacuum cleaner to its cupboard she heard, or thought she heard, the wife's whisper: 'Go on, Shane, give the old lady a hand with all that gear.'

Dorothy walked out of the church without looking back.

'That's the best church story you've told me all year,' Paul said, chuckling as he picked up his cup of coffee. 'I mean, just imagine it. The Church Warden stands up at the beginning of the service and announces: Will the person who left the piece of paper with the girl's name and phone number on it please come and see the Vicar after the service. That should liven things up all right.'

It amused me when I discovered it, Dorothy thought. But when you sneer at it like that it somehow doesn't seem funny any more.

3

If you are fortunate enough to live towards the top of the hill at Horton Fence, and if you are prepared to bring pressure to bear on the owners of the houses below you to lop the tops off their trees if they get to the point of obscuring your view, you can enjoy seeing the way the land slopes all the way down to the water. More than that, on quiet late autumn days you can see how the mist gathers and lies in the creek. Often, as this morning, the spire of Motherston church and the top part of Betty's Knoll can be seen as the only two objects rising in an almost disembodied fashion above the mist.

Ah, that's one of the real pleasures of living here, Charles Crawford said to himself, pausing on his way back from the bathroom to take in the view in all its stillness. Almost makes up for the way my joints seem to creak when I get up in the morning these days. I'm getting to be like an old engine, I need oil everywhere to lubricate me and keep me going. And I leak more than's convenient.

'Come on, old thing,' Barbara called out to him. 'You can't spend all morning gawping at the view. You asked Frank to come round to sort out the security lights, remember?'

'Oh, did I?'

'Yes, you did. And he'll probably want to call in first thing.'

'Oh, sod.' Charles dragged himself reluctantly from the window and tried to walk across the bedroom as though all his joints were functioning with perfect smoothness. He knew from experience that being called old thing probably wasn't an endearment; more likely, it was a prelude to an enquiry about which part of him was hurting and how long it had been doing so. Why does she have to watch me so closely, he thought. I'm not about to keel over. And I'm allowed to creak a bit at my age.

He sat down heavily on the bed and reached for his socks. First thing on a chilly morning, take care of your feet. But, perhaps because he was thinking too much about why he couldn't immediately remember having summoned Frank, he brushed his hand awkwardly against his toes and couldn't avoid reacting to the discomfort he had caused himself.

'Now what have you done?'

'Nothing, as far as I'm aware.'

'Well, you're making an awful lot of noise about nothing, old thing. Are you sure you haven't got another dose of gout coming on?'

Charles took a deep breath, knowing that an immediate answer would be unwise.

'Not sure yet,' he said. 'But even if I have, the pills will soon sort it out. And, in case you were wondering, I'm not such a fool as to pretend I can do without them. If I need them, I'll take them. Will that satisfy you?'

'Whatever you say, dear,' Barbara said, as she headed out of the bedroom. 'They're your feet.'

Barbara's prediction was correct; Charles was only half way through his first slice of toast when Frank arrived. Barbara therefore felt that it was up to her to go and welcome him and offer him coffee. By the time Charles had hauled himself from the breakfast table and out of the front door Frank was already busy disconnecting the outside light and muttering to himself about the state it was in.

'What's the problem?' Charles enquired, aware that he was probably sounding rather aggressive.

'Old age. All furred up.'

'Tell me about it.'

'We've all got it coming.'

'It's arrived with me already, Frank. Or that's what it feels like this morning.'

'I wouldn't worry too much, Colonel.' Frank grinned. 'A good scrape should help.'

'Just what I need, I'm sure. Doesn't always come on when it should.'

'I'm not surprised. Connections like these, you're lucky it comes on at all.'

'Can you fix it?'

'I reckon. Sensor's probably on the blink as well. This is the oldest one, that right?'

'I expect so. It was here when we bought the place. We put another one on the garage when we had it extended. That one's more reliable. But what I really wanted to ask is whether we can have another one nearer the entrance gate.'

'You can have it where you like. As long as there's something solid we can fix it to.'

'Let's go have a look, then.'

With which, Charles marched off down the driveway, telling himself that his toes didn't really hurt, and making the assumption that Frank would be following him, as good subordinates should. Frank got down off his ladder and decided that it would be wise to leave his mug of coffee, even though it had now cooled down to the temperature at which he liked drinking it.

'Problem is,' Charles announced, glancing over his shoulder to make sure that Frank was in earshot, 'with the house being a good two hundred yards or so from the front gate, the little bastards can get well inside the property without drawing attention to themselves.'

What little bastards, Frank wondered, chuckling to himself. Badgers? Jehovah's Witnesses?

'Are people getting in?'

'I wouldn't wonder. I just want a big light up somewhere here to deter them. And to light things up for us when we drive in at night.'

'It'll have to be fixed to a tree.'

'No problem. Mind you...' Charles allowed his voice to trail off.

Now what? Is he going to change his mind?

'If that wretched social housing thing ever happens, of course, we'll have to put in much more security.'

'What?' Frank said, trying to keep an even tone in his voice. 'To guard yourself against a bunch of old people with zimmer frames?'

'Is that what we're in for?'

'Nothing's for sure yet. Planning application's due in soon.'

Charles grunted.

'Mind you,' Frank observed, 'older people can misbehave, too. Look at what Betty's done to herself.'

'Betty?'

'Mrs Henshaw.'

'Ah, yes. Barbara said she saw her with her arm in plaster. What happened?'

'Fell over when she was trying to unlock her car door. Put her arm out to break her fall and ended up with a broken wrist and a cracked bone in her forearm. Someone should have stopped her even trying to get into her car. Must have been at least four times over the limit.'

'Hm, that figures,' Charles observed, hoping that the subject was now closed. Frank's a good fellow, but one always has to remember that he has very strict views on alcohol. Must be a Methodist, I suppose.

'So, Colonel,' Frank said. 'Another light here overlooking the gate, and get the one by the front door to behave itself. Is that it?'

'Yes, please. Seen all you need to? I'm getting cold.'

So am I, and my coffee will be, too.

'Give me another five minutes and I'll be able to tell you whether I can rescue the other one. Do you want a price for the new one?'

'Not to bother, Frank. You always do us a good deal.'

‘Do you think there’s any point in trying to invite Malcolm to come at Christmas?’ Dorothy asked. The end of breakfast was her preferred time to try to engage her husband in her concerns, before he vanished into some activity of his own and left her, once again, feeling excluded.

‘That sounds like a *num*,’ Paul replied, from behind his newspaper.

‘A what?’

‘Don’t you remember your Latin?’ This time he did look over the top of the newspaper. ‘It’s the word you use at the beginning of a sentence when you ask a question expecting the answer no.’

Dorothy failed to see the humour which was apparent to her husband.

‘You haven’t answered my question.’

‘I think you’ve answered it yourself. It seems to me to be rather pointless asking when we know the answer’s going to be no.’

‘It would look bad if we don’t. I don’t want us to give him the impression that we’ve given up on him.’

‘Even though we have. Is that what you’re saying?’

‘Paul, how can you say that? He’s our son!’

‘I’m rather painfully aware of that,’ Paul said, realising that he needed to placate her. ‘And I don’t enjoy rejection any more than you do. Which is why I can’t see much merit in inviting another bout of it.’

He picked up his newspaper again, but Dorothy hadn’t finished.

‘So it means we’ll be on our own again.’

‘Is that a problem? We can have a peaceful day together. No disruptive presences.’

‘I wish Harriet was still around. He would listen to her.’

Maybe Harriet didn’t care for being used as a means of keeping us in touch with Malcolm, Paul wondered. Maybe she got tired of the pressure she felt we were exerting on her.

Maybe that was one of the reasons she was willing to go and live in Australia. But it won't help if I say so. Time to change the subject.

'Had you seen this?' he asked. 'The planning application's gone in for the Church Field development and there's going to be a display of the proposals at the Village Hall on Friday and Saturday.'

'Oh,' Dorothy said, listlessly.

'That'll get the Nimbys going,' Paul commented, sounding as though he relished the prospect. 'And I expect they'll all be busy contacting the Weekend Bananas, too.'

'All right, tell me,' Dorothy said, wearily. 'What's a Weekend Banana?'

'Those who are doing their best to deaden the village by only using their houses on an occasional basis at weekends. They're often the most vociferous about proposals like this. And their rallying cry is Build Absolutely Nothing Anywhere Near Anyone.'

'I suppose we'd better go along and see what they're thinking of doing. But it's not going to make a lot of difference to us, is it?'

'It'll make the main street a mess for ages if they do go ahead. And it looks to me from what the article says that it'll be a lot of housing in a relatively small space.'

'So they can make more money?'

'Not really, if it's social housing. They won't be charging open market rents, they're not allowed to. But there'll be all sorts of arguments about why it has to be high density, I'm sure. And you can see what that's going to do for some of our friends up the road.'

'You mean...?'

'I can hear it coming already. Packing in as many undesirables as they can, and all that sort of ranting. I tell you, this one will run and run.'

Paul got up from the table, brushed his lips drily across

the top of his wife's head, and left the room. Dorothy sat where she was for a further couple of minutes, although she had finished her cup of tea, and then told herself to get up and clear the table in the hope that activity might distract her from gloomy thoughts.

But it didn't.

When did it all start to go so wrong with Malcolm, she wondered – knowing that she had asked herself this question many hundreds of times already, and that she wasn't likely to get an answer today either. He was quite obedient and amenable as a young child – much easier to handle than Harriet, who was the noisy one who was always getting into trouble.

Maybe we shouldn't have sent him to boarding school, though we didn't take the decision for him, I remember we had a long discussion about it. I know Paul thought it would be good for him because it would make him socialise more; and in lots of ways he was right, he was becoming very solitary and uncommunicative. And I honestly don't think it would have helped him, or helped our relationship with him, to have had him in the house all the time when he was fourteen or so. When we asked him how he was getting on he would just shrug his shoulders and say something along the lines of 'It's all right, I suppose.' And schools are quick to pick up on it if they can see that a boy is really struggling. When we asked, they said he seemed introspective and that he had the potential to do rather well if he was willing to push himself a bit harder. Which we knew already.

The only time he got into any trouble was when he vandalised pews with a big penknife, and tore up hymn books in the School Chapel. Not just once, he did it repeatedly. A form of rebellion against me, I suppose. But I'm not going to apologise for my faith, and even though Paul's Christianity is pretty lukewarm these days he always supported me about taking the children to church services. When the school challenged him about his behaviour they told us that he suddenly got very angry and resentful and shouted things like 'You've no right to force me to go.' When that didn't get him anywhere he declared that he had become Jewish and that he was therefore entitled to stay away from Church services. But as he valued some of his privileges as a sixth former and he was threatened with having them taken away they found a way of quietening him down.

It was only after he had finished school that he started looking at us accusingly and saying things like 'You sent me away.' Neither Paul nor I can recall him ever coming out with that whilst he was at the school. That's one of the strangest bits of the whole thing. And he was always dutiful and punctilious about remembering birthdays and sending us presents.

I imagine he may have felt resentful about Harriet, because we had a much freer and more open relationship with her – but then she made it easier for us, it wasn't as though we didn't try with him. She told us that he didn't say a lot to her, either – but she was always rather keen to deter us from trying to bring things to a head with him. She'd tell us that he had to be allowed to find his own way, and when we said that we wanted to talk to him to try and find out if we'd failed him in any way she got quite sharp with us and said 'You're trying to mould him. You mustn't.'

But we weren't, Dorothy thought, sighing as she put down her tea-towel. We did our best to be even handed in the way we treated the two of them, financially and in every other way. And we know that you have to let go when your children turn into adults, we've never tried to take their decisions for them. It would have been difficult with Malcolm anyway, as soon as he graduated he went off to work in some Government agency office in Scotland and he hardly ever came home after that. Clearly he could make friends when he wanted to, he was very rarely in when we phoned him, and I think he only once came home for Christmas, the rest of the time he 'had been invited to stay with friends here.' He never told us who the friends were, whether he had a girl-friend, anything. But we still got the Christmas cards and the birthday cards and the presents – books usually, that's always been safe ground for all of us. And we checked with him when Paul retired and we decided to move out of London, we didn't want him not to know that we were thinking of selling the home he grew up in. He just ignored our letters and our phone calls, and when Paul did finally manage to catch him in one day he simply said 'Well, that's your business, isn't it?' and hung up more or less straight away.

The really hurtful bit was when he moved to Leicester and never let us know. We sent him a cheque for his birthday and eventually our letter came back to us from Scotland just marked 'Gone Away.' Harriet knew what was going on and knew where he was living, but she refused to get involved. 'I'm sorry the relationship's broken down,' she told us. 'In fact I think he's sorry, too. But I can't mend it for you, and Malcolm wouldn't forgive me if I tried.' Which we had to accept. Harriet made some comment about him having 'issues to sort out,' but I could never find out what they were – or even if she knew properly herself. The nearest we've got to understanding was when she told us that 'I think he rather objects to your cosy life-style. He doesn't do cosy, you know.'

Am I to lose my son because I go to Church and because Paul had a settled career in the Civil Service?

I was never convinced that it would be a good idea for us to pay him a surprise visit, but in the end Paul persuaded me, as we were driving past Leicester one weekend. He argued that it was the only way of finding out what was going on as he didn't respond to messages any more. And he clearly wanted to give him a piece of his mind about being so discourteous to us and not caring about our feelings. But, of course, he never got the chance.

It still makes me wince, what happened that day – even though it must be more than two years ago now. We had to knock twice before he opened the door, and the look he gave us…I just can't get it out of my mind. One part shock, three parts sheer loathing. And then there was the girl cowering beside him – Bangladeshi, probably. She seemed quite terrified; big wide eyes, quite a bit of hair on her upper lip, a posture which suggested that she was expecting to be hit. Though there was nothing aggressive about the way he spoke to her. He just said to her, reassuringly: 'Don't worry, Riz. They'll soon be gone. I promise.'

And we were soon gone, we had no option. He told us: 'I didn't invite you, did I? When I want to see you I'll let you know. But *I'll* decide when that is. And don't ever, ever do this to me again.' And slammed the door in our faces. We heard him locking a bolt behind it.

Oh, this is no good, Dorothy said to herself. Quarter past nine in the morning, and I feel as though I could just lie down on the floor and howl. I mustn't give in. I must force myself to do something useful. I'll go and change the bed linen, even though it's a day early.

'Well, what's your verdict?'

Edward snorted, still busying himself with their drinks.

'Have you got them mixed up?' Edith asked, a few minutes later. 'There's much more gin in this than you normally give me.'

'I've given myself an extra dose, too. We'll need it, to help us recover from what we saw this afternoon.'

Edward sat down heavily in his chair, wincing slightly as he tried to choose a position to make his bad leg more comfortable.

'I found all those drawings a bit…fanciful,' Edith said. 'Difficult to imagine what real houses would look like. Though some of the ones they've built elsewhere look pleasant enough. You know, there was that bit at the far end of the hall where they showed other properties of theirs.'

'I suppose they'd do all right in Crapwell. There's plenty of that sort of stuff there already. A few more wouldn't do any harm.'

'I think I'll go and give this a bit more tonic,' Edith said. 'If you don't mind, that is.'

Edward snorted again.

'You asked for my verdict,' he said on her return. 'Well, they use sex to sell most things these days, so why not housing developments as well?'

'What…?'

'That red haired girl with the legs. I had a long chat with her. Very smooth talker. At least nine and a half out of ten for sex appeal and manipulative charm.'

'Careful, dear. Some people may feel the same way about Sandra.'

'Anyway,' Edward said, choosing to ignore this comment, 'she spun me a long yarn about how urgent it is to build more social housing in the South West because the gap between incomes and house prices is wider in this area then almost anywhere else outside Kensington and Chelsea. And how it's the County Council and the District Council who determine what's needed where, their role is just to be a responsible social landlord providing what's needed to the highest design standard they can afford, and surely I didn't have a problem with older people having a chance to downsize so that they could stay in the village, all this ever so soothing stuff.'

'It's a reasonable argument, isn't it?'

'But have you seen how closely they're all going to be packed in? I suggested to her that if the development gets built they should call it Sardine Close, but that didn't go down very well. Instead I got another lecture about how Government grant for social housing has been progressively reduced over the years so that half the money they use to build them has to be borrowed at commercial rates, and how there are strict controls on the rents they can charge, so either they get built at high density or they don't get built at all. And of *course,* she reassured me, whilst she pawed me and fiddled with the buttons on her blouse, they'd love to be able to reduce the density so that people had bigger gardens, but we both had to accept that life isn't like that, and would I like to look at the positives. Good thing Charles Crawford didn't hear that, he'd just have told her to undo the next button so that he could have a proper look at them.'

'And what does she see as the positives?'

'If there are more people in the village we've a better chance of the shop staying open, there'll be more people to take part in community activities, all that sort of stuff. She even used some ghastly phrase about how having the development would *refresh* the community. I don't want to be refreshed like that! This is my idea of refreshment.' Edward raised his gin glass, which was now almost empty.

'It'll be your idea of blood pressure, too, the way you're talking.'

'Look, you asked me what I thought, so I'm telling you. I'm sure she's right about what she says, but what we saw this afternoon simply *isn't* appropriate for Horton Fence. Or not in anything like its present form. It's out of keeping with the whole style of the village. I'm going to get Barnes to have a look at it.'

'Barnes?'

'Barrister. Acted for us on planning arguments. Always got us what we wanted. If anyone can blow the thing out of the water, he can.'

'Aren't you being a bit hasty?'

'We're only allowed three weeks to put in our comments. We've got to get started straight away.'

'Hmm...' Edith made as if to go towards the kitchen.

‘Look, my love, I’m serious about this. Either this thing gets stopped or Plan B comes back on the agenda, and I know you don’t want that to happen.’

‘Not…?’

‘Spain. Yes. Better climate, better everything.’

‘Now listen to me, Edward. If you think I’m prepared to have us uproot completely just because you’re feeling liverish about a planning application which may never happen you’d better think again. Have another gin and then do something useful, like laying the table.’

4

From Brigadier Gerald H D Farquharson, OBE

Dear Revd. Wilson

I am writing to express my considerable concern about the way in which the Church and the Diocese appear to be handling the negotiations over the sale of what used to be Lady Cuthbertson's land. As you are aware, my physical disabilities are such that I decided three years ago that it was no longer practicable for me to continue serving on the PCC, but I hope nevertheless that my views will be taken into account.

As I understand it, the Church is coming close to an agreement to hand over the land in question to the District Council in exchange for a paltry sum of money and a small parcel of land which would permit an extension of the cemetery. The District Council, in collaboration with some Housing Association of which I have never previously heard – and which has no connection whatever with the village – then intends to use the land for the construction of a preposterously large number of dwellings to house people imported from all over the place.

This is neither acceptable nor sensible. I have no idea who valued the land, but clearly he (or she) has made a botch of it – or else the Church has consented to be taken to the cleaners by the District Council, which has no doubt entered a disingenuous plea of poverty. This arrangement *must* be reviewed as a matter of urgency; I am sure I have no need to remind you of the parlous state of the Church's finances, and therefore I find it very difficult to understand why you are apparently conniving at the release of an extremely valuable asset for a sum which, in old money, amounts to roughly 31 pieces of silver.

I have already notified the planning authority of my objections to the proposed housing development, and therefore there is no need for me to rehearse them at length in this letter. In short, too many dwellings are envisaged, the building materials are inappropriate, there is insufficient off-street parking, and the implication that there is sufficient demand for all the properties from people already living within the village – whether for rent or for purchase – lacks all credibility.

There are wider issues at stake here, and they concern me deeply. The Church exists to serve the village, the inhabitants of nearby farms and hamlets, and those who visit Horton Fence. It is an essential part of the fabric of community life and it holds the potential, even in these secular days, to provide a powerful force for binding the community together for the collective good, whether or not every member of the community is a believer. Your role, as our parish priest, is to exemplify these values and to provide us with the spiritual and moral leadership to help us achieve these goals of quality living and mutual support.

Yet you and others in the Church seem to be behaving as though you have forgotten that this is your primary purpose. You spend a disproportionate amount of time and energy handing round the begging bowl so that you can provide financial support to underprivileged children in African countries whose poverty is a direct consequence of corrupt and incompetent government which the Church, like this country's government, is too pusillanimous to confront. In the latest parish magazine you urge us to engage with the homeless and with other less fortunate members of society. Has it escaped your notice that we all pay taxes to support Social Services Departments who are there to do this kind of thing?

And, worst of all, you expect us to enthuse over the new arrangements for running the Church under what you call a 'Team Ministry' – surely the most disgustingly flabby-minded piece of ecclesiastical jargon ever to be inflicted on members of the Church. Your support for this wretched housing development proposal is all of a piece with this sloppy misguided way of thinking.

I fear that, in this, you are merely following the example set by our Primate. In these days of ever dwindling Church attendance we need strong leadership and decisive stands on the major issues of the day, not woolly liberalism and endless prevarications. I say this with a direct and personal understanding of what firm leadership looks like and feels like. Does it not occur to you that this may explain why the mosques and the gurdwaras are always full whilst the churches spend most of their time being empty?

The strength of the Church of England lies in the thousands of parish churches serving and leading their individual communities. Those of us who have supported it, financially and in many other ways, throughout our lives care for it too much to allow us to stay silent when we see this strength being wilfully eroded by a focus on thinly spread and ineffectual do-gooding to the world at large. Kindly remember this – and re-adjust your focus on Horton Fence and on what needs to be done to ensure its survival as a strong and cohesive Christian community.

I should mention, in conclusion, that I have discussed this letter with my fellow Trustees. They agree entirely with what I have set out above. Your response to this letter will determine whether the Farquharson Trust will continue to support the Church as generously as it has done hitherto. I have also sent a copy of this letter to the Archdeacon.

Yours sincerely

'Well, I think that's it, then,' Margaret Wilson said, not trying to conceal her weariness. 'Unless anyone has Any Other Business?'

Horton Fence PCC meetings were rarely over in less than an hour and a half, and this one had already passed the two hour mark.

'What about Brigadier Farquharson's letter?' Barbara Crawford asked, in her usual polite fashion. 'I was rather… expecting you to bring it to the table.'

'I wasn't aware you knew about it,' the Vicar replied.

'Charles became one of the Trustees last year. I thought you might have been aware of that. So we all know what's been written. I have one or two extra copies in case anyone wishes to see them.'

'Does this mean, Vicar, that you were hoping to conceal this from us?'

'Certainly not, Mr Thomas. I'm surprised you make the suggestion.'

The undue length of the meeting had been, in large part, caused by Mr Thomas's objections to the new pattern of services which had been proposed and, despite his comments, eventually agreed.

'I am taking advice on how best to respond on behalf of the Church. You will appreciate that I need to discuss what has been said with colleagues.'

'But surely you can give us a flavour of your own thinking?' Mr Thomas insisted.

Ms Wilson took a deep breath. 'Very well, since I sense that you're not going to allow me to go otherwise. I find myself in agreement with a number of the sentiments he has expressed with such passion. Some, that is, not all. But I think Mr Farquharson should perhaps keep in mind that he does not own the Church, nor can he buy it.'

'But…'

The Vicar stood up, saying: 'I'm sorry, but the conversation is closed for the evening. You'll hear more at our next meeting, I'm sure.'

She gathered up her papers and shoved them hurriedly into her briefcase, deliberately avoiding eye contact with anybody in the room.

'You'll permit me to go home, I'm sure. I started work before eight this morning, and I didn't have time for any dinner before I came to this meeting.'

She was aware of Barbara saying 'Yes, of course' and of one or two other murmurs which sounded like assent. But only one or two.

'Yes, I think you can give me another drink,' Edith said, holding out her wine glass. 'But just make it a half. Ellie's doing her bit in the kitchen, but I'd better be around to supervise. She may put something crazy in the soup, just to see if we notice.'

Edward smiled fondly as he poured out more wine for both of them.

'As well as her hair, you mean?'

'Yes, I rather wish she'd get into the habit of tying it back, but I don't want to put her off helping.'

'And what about Laura?'

Edith allowed her eyes to roll.

'Stumped off to her room saying she couldn't bear the thought of us eating all that meat and she didn't want to be around to watch us.'

'Typical, eh?' Edward said.

'I just hope she isn't going to spoil Christmas for us all by being disruptive.'

'Oh, I don't think she will. And thank goodness she came off the idea of bringing that German girl home with her. She didn't sound like fun at all.'

'Quite. Poor girl, I wonder how she'd have been able to cope with all our lot.'

A variation of the same thought was occurring to Laura as she pounded out her e-mail. Unlike Ellie, she had soon decided to tie her long, dark hair back to prevent it from falling across the screen of her lap-top. She was lying on her bed, propped up on her elbows, and completely oblivious of the sounds of increasing jollity coming from the dining room below her.

Dear Petra

Yes, you were right not to come. I hope it's not too awful for you being back home. I can't imagine what it must be like to be in a house with parents who are at war with each other, at least *that's* not a problem we have here. If anything, it's the opposite. They all bray at each other like a bunch of self-satisfied donkeys. And right wing donkeys at that. My father actually *approves* of that unspeakable man Bush and thinks he's doing the right thing wanting to send yet more troops to die in Iraq. And the rest of them agree with him – or else they're too bored with the whole subject and all they want to talk about is horses and clothes. And babies, when all my air-headed sisters are here. I hereby solemnly swear that I will do my bit towards solving the problem of overcrowding on the planet by NOT HAVING ANY BABIES. I don't say this to any of my sisters, because I know they'd just give me the brush off by telling me that all that would go out of the window as soon as I meet the right kind of man. Well, it won't; and right now I don't want the right kind of man any more than I want the wrong kind of man.

Which brings me to what I really wanted to say to you, which is that I'm not at all upset or horrified or put off because you told me last week that you love me in the way you do. I'd thought this was so for a while, so it was great that you had the courage and the honesty to say so. And it was really rather lovely the way you embraced me and fondled me, so much pleasanter than having men panting and groping all over me. But, as you've probably guessed, I can't love you in the same way, I'm just not made like that. I've never felt any kind of sexual attraction to another woman – of any age. I want very much for us to go on being close friends, but I'm afraid a few cuddles will be the limit, and preferably with most of my clothes on. I'm sorry if I led you on last week by allowing you to undress me a bit, I was wanting to comfort you because you were upset, that's all.

Anyway, I feel better now I've said that, so back to the horrors of family life here where I'm continuing in my role as Official Black Sheep (my two older sisters are blonde and my younger one has long golden hair and I'm sorry to have to say that they're all gorgeous). Last night I really stirred it up when they all started talking about a social housing development which is planned for the middle of our village – you know, housing to buy or rent for people on low incomes. They all seem to think it's a horrific idea, and that everybody who lives in this type of house must by definition be a delinquent or a drug addict or a petty criminal – or worse. I asked them where their evidence was, and it's obvious that they haven't got any. 'We all know what goes on on those Council estates' was the best they could come up with. Pathetic!

So I told them that I thought that a social housing development was the best thing that could happen to the village, and you can imagine the reaction to that. Our village has to a large extent been taken over by people like my father who've made stacks of money in the City of London and then want to spend the last twenty years of their lives in a pretty village in the country. This pushes house prices up so high that ordinary working people with genuine local connections simply can't afford to buy a house here any more. I said I thought that was selfishness and lack of consideration gone mad, and that some social housing was needed to get things back in balance. So they all descended on me by saying that it wasn't my father's fault that house prices have got so high, and he had a right to live where he wanted after working hard for so many years.

This is where I got a bit naughty, partly to wind them up and partly because all this bigoted stuff was really starting to annoy me. I told them that I thought ours was an unsocial house because it has too much land attached to it, and if they really cared about the village the way they say they do they should allow half of it to be used to build housing for local people. The village *needs* younger people in it, I walked down to the Post Office with my Christmas cards today and I'll swear I didn't see anybody else younger than about 65!

That really got them going. My two older sisters both went at me with comments like 'How could you, Laura?' and 'Why do you always have to upset everyone?' so I decided to let it rest. My father even winked back at me, he knew what I was doing.

So, you see, I don't think this would have been your scene. Their hearts are in the right place, mainly; it's their brains I worry about. And their politics. And I wouldn't want to upset my mum seriously, she's always been a sweetie.

That's enough babble from me. Let me know how your Christmas is going.

xxxxxxxxxxxxxx

Laura

Dear Laura

Thank you so much for your message. It made me feel much better.

It is not good here. My father drinks too much and then he gets into arguments. He asked me why I do not have a boy friend. I asked him why he assumes I do not have one. If you have one, you should bring him here, he said. What, so he can see you drinking too much and being unpleasant to my mother?

He left the room after I said that. What he would say if he knew the true reason why I do not have a boy friend I cannot guess. Maybe he would have a heart attack if I told him. Maybe that is a good reason why I should tell him, what do you think?

How big is the house of your parents? It sounds a nice place.

I had a nice fantasy about you last night, but I know it can never be real.

With lots and lots of love

Petra

Dear Petra

Very quickly, because I have to go in a minute. Our house has nearly two and a half acres of land. I'm sorry I can't do that in hectares, that's because I'm an Inselaffe.

I'm flattered to know that I'm worth including in your fantasies.

Love

Laura

'Hand me a couple more of those glass angels, will you, darling?'

Valerie and Heather were decorating the Christmas tree.

'We need to make it specially nice for Grandpa,' Heather said, rather solemnly.

'We certainly do. I'm afraid it will be the last time he sees a Christmas tree.'

'Does he know he is going to die soon?'

'Yes.'

'And can't Daddy do anything for him?'

'He can't cure him, I'm afraid. He can just give him tablets to make him a bit more comfortable.'

Valerie paused in her work, deciding that she needed to concentrate on preparing her daughter for what was to come.

'You'll notice that Grandpa has changed quite a bit since the last time you saw him. He's lost a lot of weight. And he gets tired very quickly. He has a lot of pain in his stomach, even when he takes the tablets. So we mustn't do anything which tires him out even more.'

'I'm going to write a story for him,' Heather announced.

'That's a nice idea, darling,' Valerie said, sounding a bit cautious. 'Would you like to tell me what it's about?'

'Yes,' Heather said, firmly. 'It's called the Birthday Stone.' She walked across to one of the bookcases and picked up a flat, fairly round stone she had placed there earlier. 'Look,' she said. 'I shall have to write the date of Grandpa's birthday on it.'

'Ah,' Valerie said. 'Yes, I'd seen that. I was wondering where it had come from.'

'I found it in the summer on one of our school Nature Walks. It feels lovely and smooth in your hand. Try it.'

Valerie did so, aware of what a pleasant sensation it was to hold it.

'And this is what your story is about, is it?'

'Yes. It goes like this:

When the Traveller reached the shore he was helped out of the boat by a man with a beard, who was wearing a long cloak. The man smiled at him, and waved graciously at the boatman, who was already starting to take the boat back across the water.

The man reached inside his cloak and then handed a flat, round stone to the Traveller, saying: 'This is your Birthday Stone. You must look after it very carefully. Place it in your pocket, and do not take it out or look at it until you are told to do so at the end of your journey. If you find that you are getting tired, or if you are in any pain, place your hand round the stone in your pocket and ask for help to make you feel better. But only do this when you are in discomfort, do not hold the stone the whole time. You will find that there is water to drink on your journey, but there is nothing to eat until you arrive at the end. So if you start to feel hungry and weak, and it is difficult for you to go on climbing, place your hand on the stone and ask for enough strength to help you onwards.'

The man paused, surveying the Traveller.

'Perhaps it would be a good idea for you to take a stick,' he said. 'The path goes uphill for quite a bit of the way, though it never gets very steep.'

The Traveller accepted the stick without protesting. He knew that, at his age, it would be silly to pretend that he didn't need it.

'Good,' the man said, as the Traveller took the stick. He had a very peaceful and calm voice, and the Traveller felt no anxiety about the journey he was to take. 'I have told you everything you need to know. You must start your journey now, so that you can arrive at the same time as the others. Remember what I have told you about the stone, it is very important. Place your hand on it now, so that they know you are starting out.'

The Traveller did as he was told. He felt at ease, and eager to set off.

'Good luck,' the man said to him. 'The path is easy to follow.'

And having said this, the man turned away, satisfied that he had done what he needed to do to enable the Traveller to begin his journey.

The path went gently uphill, and by walking at a slow but steady pace the Traveller found that he could keep going without having to stop to regain his breath. The earth was quite bare at the beginning, but it was not long before the hillside became much greener. The Traveller saw that there were primroses and other early Spring flowers growing beside the path. Good, he thought, I've arrived at the start of things. As the path curved round to the right he was able to see the water again without turning round to look back, which he knew he didn't want to do. There was no sign of the boat which had brought him to the shore.

A little further on he became aware of the sound of animals. At first he was a little surprised, everything had seemed so quiet. But as he came round the side of the hill the path levelled out and he could see, stretching into the distance, meadows with cows and sheep grazing. There appeared to be vineyards beyond the meadows, where the land began to rise again – but they were rather far away, and the Traveller's eyesight was not as good as it had been when he was younger.

A stream crossed the path, heading down towards the meadows. On the slope above the right of the path it dropped from one stone to another, and the Traveller saw that it was completely clear. As he bent towards it he heard, or thought he heard, a voice similar to that of the man on the shore – but somehow deeper, with more authority, saying 'Yes, go on, it's safe to drink. You need to take some refreshment.'

The Traveller stood up straight again, still not sure whether he heard the voice or imagined it, but knowing that he felt fresher and stronger. He knew also that it was time to move on, though part of him wanted to sit and enjoy the scene because it was so peaceful and restful. The path became a little steeper as he made his way onwards, and for the first time he had to stop to recover his strength. The pain in his side, which had not troubled him so far, was beginning to remind him that it was part of him. He thought of placing his hand round the stone, but told himself that it was only a small problem and that he could easily live with it if he concentrated on thinking about something else.

He kept going for another few minutes, trying to distract himself by naming as many of the plants by the path as he could; but after a while he knew that he was fighting a battle which he couldn't win. Or that he couldn't win on his own, given his age. The pain had become sharper, he was finding it difficult to breathe normally, and he was beginning to feel a little dizzy. He reached for the stone, comforted by its smoothness. The voice came to him again, telling him that he could sit by the side of the path for a few minutes until he felt better again. This is the most difficult bit, the voice suggested. It gets easier after this.

For a couple of minutes he felt dazed, unclear where he was. Then his vision and his sense of where he was returned. The pain had eased, and he felt ready to continue his journey.

Two minutes later the path levelled out again and the Traveller saw that, down to his right, there was a town. He could see the market square, and the way the streets led off from it. Because of his rather dim eyesight it was difficult for him to determine whether there really were people in the market square or whether he was imagining them, because a town cannot be real if nobody lives in it. Then a thought occurred to him – in a town this size surely there should be a church? Or a mosque? He looked again, trying to persuade himself that he could see one. But the Traveller had always been a truthful man. If there wasn't one, there wasn't one. And before he had time to try to work out why there wasn't one he heard the voice again, more distinctly this time, saying: 'I don't need churches. Or any other kind of expensive buildings. The church is inside us.'

The Traveller moved on, sensing that it would be a mistake to stay and try to unravel what this meant. The path turned sharply away from the town, and it was soon hidden from view. The scenery became less interesting for a while, but as the path was nearly level, he was able to go ahead almost at a marching pace. The clouds were starting to form around the hilltops, and he knew that he had to keep moving. The one notable thing he saw was a large lake, nestling at the base of the hills. The pain returned for a moment, but soon quietened down, and he felt no need to clasp the stone again.

Because there was now little to see, and because he had been walking for quite a time, the Traveller kept his head down, concentrating on the path. He had enjoyed walking all his life, and there was something very comforting about the rhythm which you get into when you have been walking for a couple of hours or more. So he was not expecting it when the path suddenly opened out on to a kind of plateau and he realised that, for the first time since he had left the boatman and the man on the shore, he was in the presence of other people.

He saw a long wooden table, with benches on either side of it. Some people were already seated at the table; others, like himself, were just arriving and trying to work out what they were supposed to be doing. Seeing others do so, the Traveller placed his stick on the ground and moved towards the table to take one of the vacant spaces; the person next to him, whom the Traveller judged to be several years older than him, smiled pleasantly. Soon, all the places were occupied; the Traveller noticed, to his surprise, that some of the people seated at the table were quite young. He counted a total of eleven other people.

'Good. You've all done well to get here.'

The Traveller looked up, recognising the voice which he had heard more than once on his journey. He saw, or thought he saw, a man in a long cloak. Like the boatman, he had a beard – only he was taller, the beard was longer, and his voice was deeper and had more authority.

'Please help yourselves. I know you'll be hungry after your climb. There's bread and cheese, and fruit. And there's wine. But don't look for meat, there isn't any. We don't agree with killing animals.'

As soon as he heard the words the Traveller became aware of how hungry he was, and he turned his attention to filling his plate and his wine glass. The food and the wine all seemed remarkably fresh; the other guests at the table must have felt the same way, for there was hardly any conversation taking place. When he paused to look up at the man with the beard the Traveller could no longer see him, and he couldn't work out whether this was because he was standing behind him or because he wasn't there any longer. The mists which he had encountered towards the end of his journey were still in evidence, and everything was becoming slightly hazy. The Traveller wondered whether the wine was stronger than he had realised; then he heard, or thought he heard, the man's voice saying 'No, please. You've earned it. I'd like you to have some more.'

A couple of minutes later the Traveller recognised that he had eaten and drunk as much as he wished to do. He looked around, seeing that others had reached the same stage. He was about to engage the man to his left in conversation when he became aware that the man with the beard was standing directly opposite him, and was saying: 'I see you've all had as much as you wish. The table will be cleared in a minute, and then there is one final request I must make. You are to place the stones you have carried in the middle of the table. I shall need them for the people who are coming here tomorrow.'

The Traveller hardly saw the process of clearing the table, for he felt reluctant to let go of his stone. But, seeing others doing so and feeling the force of the request, he took the stone from his pocket and placed it in the centre of the table. As soon as he had done so he began to feel strangely drowsy, and unable to concentrate on what was happening around him.

He forced himself to look up. It seemed as though the other people around the table were dissolving even as he looked at them. He glanced down and saw that the same thing was happening to him. Ah, he thought; this is pleasant. It's time to let go.

And a minute later, all that could be seen were twelve stones in the middle of the table.'

'I really like that one, darling,' Valerie said. 'It's your best story yet.'

'Good,' Heather replied, sounding very matter-of-fact about it. 'I've been thinking about it for weeks.'

'There's only one thing I didn't quite understand. Why is it called a birthday stone?'

'Oh, it isn't really. It's actually a deathday stone. Only I don't think it would be kind to Grandpa if I called it that.'

'No, darling, you're right,' Valerie said, realising that she was about to cry, and burying her head in her daughter's hair as she hugged her.

5

'I've just had an e-mail from Eddie at the District Council. Apparently the people at Horton Fence are trying the Village Green objection.'

The Development Department was having its weekly meeting to review progress on all the projects which the Housing Association was trying to get going. The relaxed, rather cynical atmosphere which had prevailed whilst Howard was in charge had gone; the new Development Director, Brian Stanley, had made it very clear to his staff that there was a new regime. Three months in, the staff had become very accustomed to hearing that he had been appointed 'to raise the energy levels'. 'We're not getting a decent enough share of the development potential that's out there' had become another familiar rallying cry. But a number of the staff, who knew the Association's territory well, didn't take too kindly to being barked at by someone who had only previously worked in East Anglia.

'And what chance is there of that succeeding?' Brian asked. If an aggressive sneer had been enough to kill such an objection it would have collapsed on the spot.

'Well, they have to demonstrate that the land has been in use for twenty years for recreational purposes. It doesn't have to look like a village green, you don't have to have organised sports on it, it's enough to show that people have been walking their dogs across it on a regular basis, so…'

'Yes,' Brian interrupted. 'I know the basis of the argument. I'm asking you how strong their case is.'

'Eddie didn't say. But wouldn't it be rather difficult for us, or for the Council, to prove that they *haven't* been using it like that for years? We know the land's been vacant for a long time, and obviously it was vacant when Lady Cuthbertson was alive. We could be in for quite a delay, couldn't we?'

'Look,' Brian said, trying to control his exasperation. Some of them sounded almost pleased that the objection had been raised. 'We can sit around all day thinking negative thoughts, but that's not what we're here for. Every time you put forward a development proposal on a greenfield site someone will find a way of trying to object. And the more affluent the area, the harder they'll try.'

'They've probably hired planning lawyers.'

'Thank you. The thought had occurred to me already. Let's focus on what our next step is, shall we, instead of worrying about what the nimbys are up to? The Council wants this development to happen, and it's already given us outline planning permission. Our task is to work up a scheme to put to the Board for its next meeting. Have we got the architects' costings yet?'

'Yes.'

'What's Eddie told us about what they'll want on building materials and landscaping?'

'I need to go back to him. I think they're still trying to make their minds up.'

'What about the cost consultant?'

'We haven't asked him yet. We need to be clearer about what the Council's likely to want. I don't want to set them to work on what we've got if the Council's going to want something different.'

'And how much longer is it going to take us to find that out?'

'Eddie was off all last week with flu. And his assistant's on a management course.'

Brian took a deep breath, telling himself to resist the urge to make a snide observation. A number of his staff were, in his view, in far too cosy a relationship with the District Council officers. He wondered, in particular, about Robert

Janes. Horton Fence was in his area, and he certainly knew all the background to the project; but when it came to meetings with the District Council it seemed that he was more inclined to agree with what their officers wanted than with what made most sense for the Association. Do I need to take him to one side and remind him who he works for? Or would it be a good idea to shake up the cosiness by changing everybody's territory? No, probably not – I can't afford to lose the local knowledge. Or not yet, anyway.

'All right,' he said. 'These things are sent to try us. Remind me what mix we're going for, Robert.'

'Four two bed houses for rent, five three beds for rent, five shared ownership. Unless...'

'Unless what?'

'Unless we have to go for outright sale of one or two of the units.'

'It's a rural exception site.'

'It's still a possibility, if the Local Authority agrees.'

'Isn't it about time we made our minds up?'

'It'll be driven by the costings.'

'We've been round this loop once already, haven't we? Look, get the District Council to get off the pot, make sure the cost consultant can deliver quickly, and we'll be able to get a paper ready for the next Board meeting. Won't we, Robert?'

'Well...'

'We're not having a debate, Robert. I'm issuing an instruction.'

'Not happy, are you?'

Brian had had to leave the Departmental meeting to go to see the Chief Executive. The Development Managers were reluctant to leave the room, sensing the need to express some solidarity.

'I can't see why he's in such a tearing rush about Horton Fence,' Robert said. 'Can't he see how tricky it's going to be?'

'Targets, Robert. It's all he seems to think of.'

'The local feeling's not going to go away. We all realised that when we did the Open Day. And I've known it all along. You need consensus in this game, not bloody crusades.'

'And we need to have a very strong case to put to the Board. I understand some of them are quite nervous about this one.'

'Probably been lobbied by some of the local notables.'

'Of which there are quite a few,' Robert observed. 'Several of them gave Rosie a very hard time at the Open Day.'

'One of the Board members lives in Horton Fence, doesn't he? You know, the solicitor bloke who marches through the office when he comes here without ever saying hello to the staff.'

'No, I think it's his sister who lives there. Married to some retired Army chap. But he'll be up to speed with local opinion, I'm sure.'

The meeting was showing signs of breaking up when one of the four said: 'I wonder what the Board thinks of Brian?'

'They'll notice the difference, all right.'

'There are some pretty astute people on it these days.'

'Good,' Robert said. 'Well, I must be off. As we all know, I need to get to work.'

And, in the interests of making a point, Robert didn't leave the office until well after the rest of his colleagues had done so. He made a point of saying good night to Brian as he passed his office but Brian, concentrating on the screen in front of him, barely acknowledged the greeting.

The reason for this wasn't wholly to do with the wake up call he had handed to Robert at the meeting. After three months in the job he was no nearer to finding a house which he could expect Pam to like. Her last weekend visit, made somewhat under protest, had been not far off a disaster. She had wanted to see her sister, who was about to have another baby, but he had finally managed to persuade her to travel down so that they could look at a number of houses which he had described to her as 'all possibles.' Pam rejected all of them, with mounting contempt, and didn't even stay for lunch on the Sunday. 'If I've *got* to move you'd better make it worth my while,' she said, climbing into her car and blasting off without saying goodbye to him properly. She did relent a bit when she arrived home, giving him a reasonably friendly phone call, but since then he had adopted the habit of sending her an e-mail rather than phoning her when he was feeling tense and he knew there was a risk of their falling out with each other again.

So when Robert put his head round the door Brian was in no mood to be distracted from the message he was sending his wife:

Darling

Another not particularly great day at the office, I hope yours has been better. None of the projects I've inherited seem to be moving forward. I know there are always a lot of hoops you've got to jump through, but they seem to have twice the normal number of them down here. And the staff seem to have no sense of urgency about anything. If developments happen, that's fine, if they don't – well, that's just the way of things, they get paid the same whatever happens.

I'm beginning to think I've been brought in to do the difficult bits of the Chief Executive's job, as well. He hauled me out of a meeting today to chew me up because one of the tenant representatives had been grumbling to him about me. Said I was 'openly contemptuous' about their views as to what should be specified in our design briefs. Trouble is, these people seem to live on some strange planet where money grows on trees, they just go deaf when I try to explain to them that grant levels are going down and down, and this means we can't plan for everything we'd like to include.

Someone has to explain the realities of life to them, all the Chief Exec. seems to want to do is placate them the whole time. He told me that one of his 'absolute top priorities' was to make sure we come out well when we're inspected on how well and how fully we're involving tenants, and that I must handle things in a way which doesn't jeopardise this.

Anyway, that'll do for letting off steam. I hope there'll be something worth reading from the estate agents when I get home, one of them tried to ring me today but I couldn't take the call.

Love you lots

Brian

'You're shaking your head,' Dorothy observed.

She and Paul were sitting, as ever, in silence as they had their mid morning coffee.

'I've just found out that Turner's dead,' Paul said, gesturing at her with a magazine he had put down on the table.

'Turner?'

'Oh, nobody you knew. Just a name to me after all these years, too. I'm afraid I've reached the age where the main thing I look at is the obituaries when this thing arrives' – Paul held up the magazine, so that she could see that he was talking about his old school journal – 'and Turner was my fag, for heaven's sake.'

'So what age was he?' she enquired, feigning an interest she didn't really feel.

'Oh, sixty-four, I expect. Four years younger than me, by definition. Silly thing is, your perception of people gets frozen in time. Because I can only think of him in the context of him being my fag, somehow he's still fourteen in my mind. Ridiculous, isn't it? Became an accountant, married twice, second time to a South African. Spent the second half of his life managing a big winery.'

'So he did all right for himself?'

'Sounds like it. Anyway, I must go down to the Post Office.'

'Whilst we've still got one.'

'Oh, I wouldn't be so fatalistic about it.'

'They were sounding pretty mournful about things last time I was in.'

'Is that what they call playing the sympathy vote?'

'Oh, Paul, how can you say that? They both try their hardest to make a go of it, and I don't think the village supports them nearly as much as it should. And the Government's not helping either, telling them they can't do TV licenses any longer.'

Paul put down his magazine, recognising that it might be a good idea to say something to placate her.

'I learned a lot about Government and how it likes to operate, all those years I worked for it. I can't say I ever noticed that being helpful was one of their priorities.'

'Well, they certainly aren't being at all helpful about this. Think about what it'll mean, especially to all the older people in the village, if the Post Office has to shut.'

'I suppose, as an older person myself, I'd better start thinking about this.'

'Oh, Paul, don't be so smug. You know I'm not talking about people like us. We can drive to Clapwell, or Exeter, any time we want. And when we decide to give up driving it won't hurt us financially to go by taxi. There's lots of people in the village who can't afford to do that.'

'I suppose you're right. But it hasn't happened yet.'

'It'll be too late when it does happen. We need to start supporting them now.'

'Hm.'

'No, you can't simply brush it aside like that. Ken and Brenda are decent people, they're doing their best to provide what the village wants, and most of the village just takes them for granted.'

'I think the village might take to them a bit more if they didn't look so grumpy the whole time. Retailing's about showing an interest in your customers, you know.'

'And another thing, which might explain why you and others think they're looking hard done by. They were honest enough to say that they think the social housing development would be a good thing for the village. And not just because it would give them some more customers. They think the village has changed because of the incomers, and that this would restore the balance a bit. It's supposed to be for local people, you know. They're not the only people who think that way, either, from what Ken was saying. Apparently that very pleasant school teacher, Mike Somebody, thinks it's a good idea – and he lives right opposite where they'd be built.'

'And are you telling me that these sorts of views are not welcome in some quarters?'

Dorothy surveyed her husband before replying: 'Don't miss a trick, do you?'

'And are you going to tell me who's holding their views against them?'

'No. Work it out for yourself. And if you're going down there, don't let me hold you up.'

Edward put the phone down, muttering to himself angrily, and went in search of his wife to impart the news he had just received. She wasn't in the kitchen, or the utility room; in the end, prompted by hearing a noise from upstairs, he discovered her putting away some ironed bed linen.

'Ah, found you at last,' he said, hauling himself into the bathroom.

'Bad leg day?'

'You know it doesn't like cold damp weather.'

'Anything else it doesn't like?' Edith enquired, recognising some familiar symptoms.

'I've just found out why Byron didn't show up this morning. He's been up before the magistrates because of some drunken brawl in Crapwell just before Christmas.'

'And?'

'They've put him on probation. And I've just suffered an earful from his mother about him not really being the culprit at all, it was all the fault of the others he was with.'

'She might well be right. I don't see Byron as a leader, do you?'

'No, of course not. To be honest, he's about as much use as a fart in a colander. And I told his mother exactly what I thought about failing to let us know he wasn't coming. Frankly, Edith, it's about time we got rid of him and found somebody reliable instead.'

'He's all right if you handle him the right way. And he needs help.'

'And a good hard kick up the arse three times a day after meals.'

'I want us to go on supporting his mother. She's on her own with three of them to bring up in that tiny little Council house. Think what that must be like.'

Edward grunted.

'I think I'd better have a word with her. You probably frightened the life out of her.'

Edward withdrew, not wishing to enter into a debate about Byron's family circumstances. He limped downstairs into his study, took out his pipe and began to fill it, and switched on the TV on his desk. Once he had packed the pipe to his satisfaction – something which should never be done in a hurry, he always told himself – he lit up and turned to the stock market prices on the Ceefax.

A few minutes later Edith came into the room, brushing at the smoke with her hand.

'How can you possibly read what's on the screen through all that fug?'

‘Not a problem,’ Edward assured her, sounding much more genial now that he was engaged in one of his favourite occupations.

‘Anyway, I’ve just spoken to Byron’s mother. She was ever so contrite about having upset you, and said nothing like this has ever happened before and she was too ashamed to ring to tell us beforehand, and Byron had promised her he wasn’t having anything to do with the friends he was with any more, and how much she appreciated us employing him and so on. So I said we’d overlook the incident and he’ll be here as usual next week.’

‘Flannel.’

‘Edward, we mustn’t chuck him out. And now he’s seeing a probation officer I’m sure he’ll learn to smarten up a bit.’

‘You reckon?’

Edith recognised that it might be a good idea to change the subject.

‘And are we richer or poorer today?’

‘Not a lot’s happening. Except I’m enjoying the way they don’t check their messages for typos. I’ve just discovered that sales of mobile pohones were disappointing in the pre-Christmas period.’

Edith smiled, pleased to see him in a better humour again.

‘Still not as good as the one my mother once told me about,’ Edward went on.

‘Mm?’

‘It was when she was doing credit control work. She had to write her letters out in longhand and give them to some little typist girl. You’ll recall what a very rounded style of handwriting she had?’

‘I do. Her letters to us were always beautifully written.’

‘Yes, but they confused the typist all right. The letter came back for her to sign saying ‘Another mouth has passed and we have still not received your payment.’

Edith chuckled, and then said: ‘Whilst you’re looking at

that thing, can you let me know what the weather's going to be like tomorrow? Caroline wants me to go over and help her with the children.'

'Then you'd better be careful. There could be some feezing frog.'

'Not down here, surely?'

'No, more likely in Wolverhampton. Good idea, that. It'd help shroud the place from view.'

'And what's in store for us here?'

'Just heavy clodd, I expect.'

'Oh, I give up,' Edith said with a smile, turning to go.

'Sounds like Byron,' Edward called after her.

Paul Preece, having had to get up as usual around four o'clock in the morning to empty his bladder, was finding it difficult to settle back to sleep again. The problem with the act of getting out of bed and going next door was that it woke you up properly. Which set the mind going, and Paul's was as active as it had always been; if anything, even more so – because, in retirement, you have the advantage of setting your own agenda. No more going to the office and having to do what the rules required. Ideal for an intelligent man still in good health.

Except that the mind can sometimes be too active for its own good. Paul shifted to a different position, annoyed because he felt wide awake but knowing that he didn't want to wake Dorothy, who often started her day full of care and woe – and whose morning woe levels increased sharply if she hadn't had enough sleep. His thoughts made their way back to Turner, and he tried to accustom himself to the idea that he was now the late Edmund Turner. But the image of Turner as a fourteen year old was the only one which had any meaning for him. A big boy for fourteen, with glasses and messy, usually unwashed, fairish hair.

No, not just Edmund Turner, Paul suddenly remembered. Edmund Richard Christopher Turner. What a set of initials to wish on your son. Priapic, or what. And he lived up to it, too. Paul gasped, as a thoroughly unwelcome memory came back to him. For a moment, he feared he might have woken Dorothy, so strong was his reaction.

Why did I read that magazine, all this was safely buried until I found out about his death. Well, they say that as you get older you remember less and less of what you did recently and more and more of what went on in your childhood and your adolescence. I could do without this, though.

One day Turner had knocked at Paul's study door and entered bearing a pair of shoes he'd cleaned. Paul noticed he'd done a rather casual job on them but he noticed something else, too.

'You've got an erection,' he said.

'Mm,' Turner said, casually, surveying the bulge in his trousers. 'Happens a lot.'

'May I feel?' Paul asked and, without waiting for an answer, placed his hand there.

He felt Turner's penis stiffening further and his own springing up in immediate response. Then, a moment later, he took his hand away, saying: 'No, I mustn't. I'm sorry. You must go. I shouldn't have done that.'

He deliberately looked away as Turner left. He heard him say – or, fifty-one years later, thought he had heard him say: 'That's all right. I can handle this myself.'

And, half a minute afterwards, Paul had looked cautiously round his study door to see if there was a waiting group of younger boys outside. Which, to his relief, there wasn't. So no honey trap there – though, Paul thought bleakly, I don't suppose that phrase had been invented then.

But he knew he wasn't a popular prefect. Words like righteous, and stuffy, were applied to him. One evening, when he went to bed an hour after the younger boys, as was his privilege as a prefect, he discovered that his bed linen had been totally unmade; the sheets and blankets were all folded up and laid neatly across the mattress as all boys were directed to do on the last day of term. Worst of all, his much used dirty handkerchief had been placed on top of the pile. Paul had fled downstairs in horror to find a colleague to help him remake the bed and fend off any further humiliations which the younger occupants of the dormitory might have had in store for him.

Paul shuddered, trying to convince himself that everybody must have had equally embarrassing experiences in adolescence, and that there was nothing to get worked up about over this incident which had suddenly surfaced again. But, somehow, this convenient rationalisation refused to work. There was a carry-over into his adult life, wasn't there? Called repression. And anxiety. And a feeling that somebody, somehow, was watching and disapproving. And calling him a failure.

He and Dorothy had both been equally nervous and reticent about their relationship as man and wife. A whole new area for both of them, and neither willing to admit to the extent of their ignorance, or their fear of disappointing each other. So any words, and there were never many, which were shared in bed, were usually along the lines of 'no' and 'don't, please' and 'not there'. After a while Paul grew tired of trying, and he suspected that Dorothy was secretly relieved. Making love became a task, not a pleasure – particularly as she wasn't able to conceive exactly when she had planned to do so. But they got there, in the end, and after that the exertions of looking after small children took up all their spare energy – most notably in the case of Harriet, who only seemed to need half the amount of sleep which a normal child required.

Paul shifted his position once more, aware that his left arm was uncomfortable because he had been putting too much weight on it. I'm not surprised that Dorothy was so peevish with me this morning, he thought. She might not recognise it, but I'm sure it's a lifetime of disappointment and frustration showing through. Maybe if I'd been more use to her sexually she'd feel more relaxed and fulfilled now.

No, he told himself, shifting position once again, that's nonsense. She's always had a strong sense of duty. When she was doing social work she actually chose to work with older people, it wasn't forced on her.

Duty, eh? I'm not sure exactly what it means. Obligation, yes – but that's different, it means fulfilling your side of the contract. They're not the same thing, are they? Did I have a duty to her, sexually, or an obligation? Oh, I don't know, I'm tying myself in knots. Let's be honest and say it wasn't fun, the way it should have been and could have been. And I regret that, I really do.

But that's all in the past, I can't do anything about it now. I've always been more interested in things of the mind than things of the body. Dorothy knew that when she married me, she said it was one of the things which made her feel safe with me. And we've had a safe life, so what's the matter with that? Malcolm deciding to go all strange wasn't part of the script, but we've got to let that run its course. Dorothy needs to learn to stop fretting about it, though it's no good my saying so. I was trained how to be detached years ago, it comes easily to me. I know it's a lot harder for her.

Ah, where did all this train of thought start? With Turner, didn't it? And his erection. So why didn't I carry on? He wouldn't have minded. And I'd have enjoyed it. After all, what was I thinking about when the dirty handkerchief was brought into use? Girls didn't feature in my world then at all. I knew they existed, but they were completely alien. I hadn't even begun to think about how to approach a girl – socially, sexually or anything.

Oh, this is no good, Paul said to himself. I want to get back to sleep. I'll leave all this stuff alone and think about something worth thinking about. I'll count how many villages I can name between here and Exeter. Shall I start by going north to Crapwell and Old Mellort? I really must find out how that place got its name. Or perhaps I should start with Motherston and then work my way up to Lower Yarling and Upper Yarling? If I go that way I get to Beddlesworth and then the Bringhams. A bit to the east there's a tiny place called Dintry, I think. No, maybe it's Daintry......

6

'It was good to see the church so full,' Edith said. The lady next to her was definitely not a local, she had decided. And she appeared to be on her own.

'Is that not normally the case?'

There was no mistaking the tone of disapproval in the question.

'For ordinary services, no.'

'Why not? Vicar no good?'

'She tries hard.'

'Oh, one of them. Had one at our church once. Didn't last long.'

They were able to move forward to collect something to eat from the buffet table. Edith was relieved to get away from her companion and went in search of someone more familiar.

'Poor old Farquhy,' she said to Barbara. 'The village won't be the same without him.'

'You're right. Even though he's not been seen for years.'

'Must have been a relief to him to be able to go.'

'I expect it was. I gather he was beginning to lose it a bit, mentally.'

'Mm. Sad. Could have been the effect of the painkillers.'

Mrs Henshaw arrived, clutching a glass of something fizzy. Edith had assumed that there was only tea and coffee to drink.

'Very good address,' she asserted. 'Do we know who the vicar is? Some Army connection, no doubt.'

'Must have been. He clearly knew him quite well.'

'I'm very vague about Farquhy's family circumstances,' Edith said. 'I gather his wife died a long time ago.'

'That's right,' Barbara replied. 'One day she was as fit as

anything, next day she had a massive brain haemorrhage. It was only about a year or so after they moved here. He never really recovered from the shock of losing her.'

'Only you wouldn't have known it. Kept his feelings buttoned up,' Mrs Henshaw said.

I'm not sure I'd want to disclose too many feelings when you're around, Edith thought. I'd never know where they might end up.

'And do we know what'll happen to the house?' she asked.

'It'll probably be sold and turned into more bloody social housing,' Mrs Henshaw suggested. And, having delivered herself of this verdict, she moved away, empty glass in hand.

'Well, that's one option, I suppose,' Barbara said, smiling rather mischievously. 'But I think not, somehow. There are two sons and a daughter. As well as the niece who spent so much time looking after him. Should help their finances when the place is sold.'

'It's enormous, isn't it? It's only the second time I've ever been inside the house. And there must be, what...five acres of grounds?'

'At least.'

'But it feels all sad and musty and shut up, doesn't it?'

'Certainly does. Charles said he only ever used the kitchen and the study when he was downstairs. So I suppose this is the first time in years that this room's been put to any use.'

'Sad. It could still be a splendid house if it got some attention.'

'Needs a woman's touch.'

'And I assume there weren't any more women in his life after his wife died?'

'It appears not. I don't think he was ever at ease with other women. Or else he held it against them because they were still alive when his wife wasn't.'

'Poor old Farquhy. All that activity and achievement earlier in his life, and then he had to end up more or less as a prisoner, and all by himself most of the time.'

'A lot of his Army colleagues kept in touch. And he was a great letter writer.'

'Oh yes,' Edith said, brightening up a bit. 'We've all been on the receiving end of some of them.'

'And he was still potting away at some of his favourite targets right up to the end.'

'It's still sad, though. I know the vicar asked us to celebrate his life, but that's not how I feel, coming here to this big, gloomy place.'

'Mm. I know how you feel.'

'Or maybe it's because it's February, and it's grey and cold outside. Worst month of the year, for me.'

'My first crocuses are in bloom,' Barbara said.

But if Edith heard her she showed no sign of having done so, seeming to be deep in her own thoughts.

'I'm trying to remember the quote,' she said. 'Is it – every man's death diminishes me?'

'Oh, it's no good asking me, dear,' Barbara said. 'I'm hopeless at that kind of thing.'

'It's something like that, I'm sure. That's how I feel about Farquhy's passing, anyhow.'

'Any man's death, actually.' Paul Preece had joined them. 'It's from the famous passage which begins 'No man is an island' and ends up with 'Never send to know for whom the bell tolls; it tolls for thee.'

As this failed to provoke a response he went on: 'The bit I struggle to remember comes in the middle, and it seems rather appropriate for today. Something about 'a manor of thy friends' being washed away.'

'I think we're far enough up from the water for that not to be a problem,' Barbara observed, briskly.

'Well, it may not be washed away, literally,' Edith said. 'But in another sense that's what's happened. And I feel diminished by that. In fact the whole of the village is diminished.'

'Ah, there you are,' Charles exclaimed, marching up to them. 'Time to stop looking gloomy. I've just been having an excellent conversation with these good people, and I want to bring you in on it.'

Edith saw that he had Edward and Mr Thomas in tow, together with a number of what she assumed to be the Army mourners – including the rather militaristic lady she had encountered at the buffet table. She noticed also that he and others had glasses of whatever fizzy drink it was in their hands.

'We've been exchanging ideas about how to do something that will commemorate old Farquhy in a way which would make him proud of us.'

'And?'

'We're going to have a real, proper campaign against the social housing development. Mr Thomas has agreed to act as co-ordinator. We want as many people in the village to be mobilised against it as we can get. I don't believe anyone really wants it, but if we don't get our act together soon it'll happen by default.'

'That's what we did in our village when they threatened us with wind turbines at the top of the hill,' the militaristic lady said. 'Killed it stone dead. They'll never have the nerve to try it again. What's more' – she glared at Paul Preece, having noticed the disbelieving expression on his face – 'the whole thing was a tremendous boost to the community. Got people off their arses. Got them talking to each other. Real sense of purpose.'

'Do you know what?' Charles said, radiating enthusiasm. 'Moira tells me they were so successful at it that they've written a How to Do It guide which they sell to any other towns and villages which find they've got the same sort of threat on their hands.'

'Your village has got a lot in common with ours,' Moira said. 'Just needs someone to stir them up. You'll be amazed what you can achieve. And you'll regret it for ever if you don't make the effort.'

'It could be divisive,' Edith suggested.

'And it could be the best thing Horton Fence has done in years,' Moira retorted.

'Well, my mind's made up,' Charles stated. 'We'll do it for Farquhy. Won't we?'

Moira looked round to see where Paul Preece had got to, hoping to glare him into submission. But he had moved off to talk to another group of visitors, who were enquiring how the village had got its rather curious name.

'Is it a rabbit proof fence?' a blonde woman asked him, giggling.

Paul looked blankly at her.

'It's an Australian film,' the woman said.

'Oh.' Paul's expression seemed to suggest that he would need a great deal of persuading that Australians were capable of making films.

'It doesn't have anything to do with fences, in the sense that you and I understand the word,' Paul went on. 'In the same way, the village of Sixpenny Handley has nothing to do with coinage. There were apparently a couple of Saxon chiefs called Sax and Penna, that's where that name comes from.'

'Well, I never knew that.'

'The derivation of our village name is quite similar. There appears to have been a Saxon or possibly a Norman landowner called Venn or Fenn. And most of the original village was built towards the top of the hill, so on old maps you can see it shown as Fenn's High Town. Then, and this is the interesting bit, at some stage the order of the words got reversed, so the High Town bit came first. And then you can see how it got gradually changed into Horton Fence. What I'm trying to do in my researches is to identify exactly when the change occurred, and why. There's a gap of nearly eighty years between the latest mention I've found of the old name and the earliest mention of the current one. It's frustrating when you find that the documentation's so sketchy.'

Paul was about to embark on an account of the various unproductive lines of enquiry he had followed up over the past year when he realised that his audience had started to drift away.

'You're worn out, aren't you?'

Edith had come in to say goodnight to her youngest daughter; she could see that Ellie was longing to tell her about her weekend but that she was having extreme difficulty in not dropping off to sleep halfway through her story.

'I had a great time.'

'But you didn't get much sleep last night, by the look of it.'

'Sandra and Ollie took me to this great gig, then when we got home we played some more discs, then today we went to a party at this fabulous penthouse flat in Docklands. It's all glass windows and you can see for miles.'

'I hope you weren't drinking anything you shouldn't have been.'

'I certainly wasn't. Someone gave me a bit of bubbly with my orange but it tasted horrid so I put it down again.'

Edith leaned forward to stroke away one of the long strands of golden hair which had fallen across Ellie's face.

'I love going to Sandra's, Mummy. And Ollie's just, well mmm!'

'Now, listen to me, Eleanor Jackson-Wright,' Edith said, with mock severity. 'You are thirteen years old, I'm taking you back to school tomorrow, and you've no business making comments like that about your sister's husband. What's more, I think it might be a nice idea if you spent a bit more time with your other sisters when you come home.'

Ellie screwed her nose up in disapproval.

'When you go to Caroline's it's all wet nappies and runny noses and keep your voice down.'

'Yes, I know what you mean, darling. It'll get better as they get a bit older.'

'And Laura's…like…'

'Mm?'

Ellie sat up in a bed as a sudden thought came to her.

'Mummy, are you sure Laura's my sister? She's so different from the rest of us.'

'Ellie! Really!'

'She's just…loopy.'

'She takes after your father. Very bright, lots of energy, lots of charm, and as obstinate as you'll ever meet. That's why your father made such a success in his business career. He had an idea and he stuck with it when everybody told him he'd never make a go of it. And he was right. Though I understand what you're saying about Laura, she can get a bit trying when she's on one of her crusades, can't she?'

But Ellie had already fallen asleep half way through this little lecture.

Edith continued to sit on the side of her bed for a few minutes. She really is going to turn out to be the best looking of all of them, she thought – and it's not just the stunning gold hair. Everything about the structure of her face is perfect, and her teeth are just as they should be. And to think how horrified we were when we found out that she was on the way, we really did think seriously about having her aborted. What we'd have missed!

Edith realised that her vision was getting blurred. She wiped her eyes and withdrew quietly from the bedroom.

Charles closed the front gate of Mr Thomas's house carefully behind him and set off to walk the quarter mile uphill to his own home. I can see why he's so determined to stop the housing development, he thought; it would completely ruin the outlook from his house, and from the three either side of it. And I don't think he's being unreasonable about objecting, at all. He told me, very quietly, that his wife tends to suffer from depression – partly because she's getting increasingly arthritic and can't get about much – and he fears that her condition will get a lot worse if there's to be a lot of noisy building across the road from them and they'll end up losing most of their view. I can't say I particularly like his drab, modern house but it's their choice and they're obviously very proud of it. 'We didn't spend all that time saving up to retire to a pleasant place in the country just to have it ruined by this kind of thing' he told me – and I could really hear the bitterness in the way he said it. Not the kind of man I'd ever want to have much to do with, socially, but that's not the point. This is an issue for the whole of the community, so we need everybody's viewpoint; and a lot of them seem remarkably similar.

What's more, I admire his tenacity, Charles thought, pausing for a moment where the road started to get steeper. He's managed to make contact with just about all the people who have houses they only come to at weekends. They don't get a chance to come to Parish Council meetings, so how are they to have their say about this wretched development? I wouldn't want the village to have too many weekenders, but you have to accept that it's a lifestyle many people choose. And they've got as much right as those of us who live here the whole time to have their voices heard. As far as I understand it from what Thomas was saying, a number of them won't be keeping their London flats for much longer anyway, they're getting so concerned about the Islamists and what they get up to. So we must keep their views in mind and not regard them as second class members of the community, as I suspect some people in the village tend to do.

Most interesting that the District Council has deferred a decision on giving planning permission, so there's still hope that the whole thing will go away – or at least that it'll get changed to something more acceptable. Some legal challenge, apparently; I must ask Edward about it. Thomas said that he could 'just about live' with a development of bungalows across the road – and if the idea is to provide for older people wouldn't this be a better idea anyway? What I really object to is that we're having somebody else's agenda foisted on us. And Moira was quite right; if we don't hurry up and make our views known the whole thing will happen by default. And it didn't help that the Parish Council simply sat on the fence. If they think they're doing their job properly by just 'referring a number of issues back to the District Council for clarification' maybe it's time we got some Parish Councillors with backbone instead.

He walked on, a little more slowly, pondering the tactical options with such concentration that he only just noticed in time that his neighbour and her daughter were about to pass him. Hurriedly, he acknowledged them – but the wife gave him such a tiny, unsmiling nod in return that he wondered why he had bothered greeting them. Strange, silent, unsocial woman, he thought. And I wouldn't even recognise the husband if I met him, even though he's been living here for nearly three years. Still, I suppose you have to accept that some people will always do more for the community than others.

And fancy James suddenly taking an interest in the issue, that really did come as a surprise. This kind of thing must seem to belong to a world so totally different from the one he's chosen to live in, but he really does seem to want to do what he can to help. Barbara and I have never quite believed him when he says how much he enjoys getting away from the frenzy in the City when he comes here. But he always seems to be pretty keen to get back to it. Or maybe that's because of his overdressed wife. Some day I'll force her to go for a five mile walk through a lot of muddy fields full of inquisitive cows. Then she might begin to see how artificial her way of life is. Mind you, she could be rather tasty looking if only she'd eat properly. That type of thin, heavily made-up girl never looks good beyond her thirties.

Charles marched along his driveway, his good humour fully restored and his breathing coming more easily now that he was on level ground again. He was aware of the smell of coffee being brewed as he entered the kitchen. Barbara and Edith were clearly having an earnest discussion about something, so all he got from his wife was a wave of the hand and a comment that there might be some left for him. There'd better be, he thought; one might have expected Thomas to offer me a coffee, but that's clearly not his style.

He managed to get about two thirds of a cup from the cafetiere, and was wondering whether he should take it somewhere else in the house when Barbara asked: 'Good meeting?'

'Excellent,' Charles replied, sounding deliberately hearty because he didn't like the careworn look on their faces. 'Old Thomas has really got stuck into it.'

'Might distract him from making life uncomfortable for the vicar,' Barbara said.

'Oh. Isn't he allowed to do both?'

'I don't think being agreeable comes easily to him. Still, if you've spent thirty years working for Health and Safety it must be hard to kick the habit.'

'Hm. Could be. How's Edward? I haven't seen him for a while.'

'Not good,' Edith replied. 'He's had a cold that turned into bronchitis, his leg doesn't like this cold damp weather, he's ratty about everything and he keeps banging on about going to live somewhere warmer. I decided to invite myself over for a change of atmosphere.'

'Good thinking,' Charles said.

'Only it seems as though nobody's having a good time at the moment. Barbara's just been telling me what happened to Dorothy Preece.'

'Oh. She hasn't told me.'

'Yes, I have. But you were listening to the cricket, so you didn't pay any attention.'

'Oh, yes, wait a minute. She had a fall when she was doing something in the church. There, see, I was listening.'

'I suppose you get half a point for that,' Barbara observed. 'She slipped on a newly polished floor in the nave and knocked herself so hard against the end of a pew that she's cracked at least two ribs.'

'Ouch. And there's nothing you can do except wait for it to heal, is there?'

'Exactly.'

'Well, maybe it'll make that husband of hers get his nose out of his history books and do something helpful instead.'

'That doesn't sound very charitable, Charles.'

'Oh. Got it wrong again, have I? Mind you, talking about people not having a good time, I just passed Mrs Thing from next door walking down into the village with her daughter and they both looked as grim as anything. Hardly said hello.'

'Oh, Charles, really! Valerie's father's just died of cancer and Heather's having a horrid time at school.'

'Why's that? I thought she was supposed to be a bright girl.'

'That's part of her problem. She's a dreamer, doesn't join in with what the others do. So she gets bullied.'

'But she's getting to be a big girl now. Surely she's worked out how to stand up for herself?'

Barbara sighed.

'Charles, dear,' she said, wearily. 'It's easy to say that. But some people don't find it easy to do.'

Charles grunted.

'Even young soldiers get bullied, if we're to believe what we hear on the news.'

'I think you'll find that's been blown up out of all proportion, because it makes a good story. They're being tested, I'd say. To see what they're made of.'

Edith pushed her chair back and got up, saying that Edward would be grumbling harder than ever if she didn't get back to him soon. Just as she was about to leave the room Charles suddenly remembered part of his conversation with Mr Thomas and asked her if she knew the latest about the legal challenge to the housing development.

'No, but I'll ask him,' she said. 'Actually, I think that's causing part of his rattiness, I gather it's not going the way he wants.'

Extract from the minutes of the Board Meeting held on 22 March, 2006:

Mr Stanley introduced a proposal to build a total of fourteen properties at Church Field, Horton Fence. Members were shown a site plan and architects' drawings of the proposed development, which consisted of four two bedroom houses for rent, five three bedroom houses for rent, and five shared ownership houses. He said that this was the first opportunity which the Association had been able to gain to work with the District Council in question, and that he was keen to move ahead as soon as practicable in order to give effect to what he saw as a new and important working relationship. He also reminded Members that the Association had come in for some criticism from the regulator for having fallen short of its planned target for delivering new homes in the previous year, and asked for approval of the proposal subject to final planning consent, which was still awaited.

Commenting on the proposal, Mr Harrison said that he knew the Horton Fence area well, and that he was sure officers were aware of the strength of adverse feeling locally. Whilst he accepted that the Association should not allow its investment decisions to be swayed unduly by the views of what was probably just a vocal minority he felt that not enough evidence had been given in Mr Stanley's paper to convince him that Horton Fence was the best location for the development. He offered the suggestion that Motherston, which was a larger community with a somewhat different and generally less affluent population mix, might provide a more appropriate location. Mrs Ormerod, in supporting these views, said that it was important that the Association's first development with this District Council should be a soundly based one. If it were to prove controversial and unpopular the Association might find it difficult to gain further opportunities in the area.

Mr Stanley explained that site availability was a crucial determinant. Following protracted negotiations the District Council had managed to obtain the site on favourable terms and was making it available at nil cost to the Association. Because there was no land cost involved it had been possible to design the houses to a high specification so that, in appearance terms, they would fit in well with nearby properties. He pointed out that, even with the design enhancements which had been incorporated following comments made at the Open Day, the project still met the Association's financial criteria.

Dr Weller said that he was concerned about the possibility of a legal challenge to the use of the site for social housing purposes, and suggested that the paper had been rather less than candid in informing Members of the potential seriousness of the situation. He had noted the problem about falling short of delivery targets but offered the view that this had been caused, at least in part, by projects not going ahead as quickly as anticipated because there had been outstanding planning and other issues to resolve at the time Board approval had been given. He said that the Board had to strike the right balance between enabling new projects to go ahead and ensuring that the way was clear for them to do so. In this instance he felt that, rather than helping the Association to catch up with its delivery targets as Mr Stanley had outlined, there was a real risk that this particular project might make the slippage worse; he said that he was therefore reluctant to agree with the proposal until the legal position had been clarified. In reply, Mr Stanley said that he had deliberately not said much about the legal challenge because he was confident that this was merely a delaying tactic which was bound to fail. The Association's solicitors had asked for Counsel's opinion, and a final answer was expected before the end of the month.

After further discussion the Board agreed to refer the proposal back to the Executive for further consideration and asked for the proposal to be re-worked in the light of:

(a) clarification of the legal entitlement to use the site for social housing

(b) an assessment of site availability in Motherston

(c) an updated Housing Needs survey.

7

'Did you know that this meeting about the housing development was going to happen?' Dorothy asked.

Mid morning coffee at the Preece household tended to be a silent affair unless she managed to engage Paul's interest in something. He had taken to making the coffee after her accident at the church but he seemed to think that, having done so, he was entitled to deliver it to her and then immediately disappear behind the pages of The Times.

'Mm?'

'This notice you just brought in. About the public meeting next week.'

'Ah, yes. I had heard mutterings when I was at the Post Office.'

'Well, come on. Put that paper down, can't you. This could be very important.'

Paul did as she had asked, and then studied the notice more thoroughly than he had done when he had collected it from inside their front door. He had not got there quickly enough to be able to see who had delivered it.

'Friday evening, I see. Timed so that the weekenders can get here and have their say.'

'We're not doing anything, are we? I think we should go along.'

'I'm not sure about that,' Paul said.

'Why not?'

'Well, for a start, look at the way it's been set up. Charles Crawford's taken it upon himself to chair it, which means it'll be packed out with objectors. It won't be an open debate at all. It'll just be a ranting session for all the nimbys. I don't think I want to be part of that.'

'You're making rather a lot of assumptions, aren't you? Look, it says it's an opportunity for the whole of the community to have their say and to make their views known to the District Council before it meets to decide on the planning application. Why should you take that to mean that there won't be an open debate?'

'Partly because I heard what Crawford was saying about it at Farquhy's funeral. And partly because he's clearly trying to usurp the Parish Council. Most of the meeting'll be taken up with people bashing the Parish Council for not having objected to the proposal. I'd rather stay away from that kind of thing.'

'Do you really think people are as mean minded as that?'

'Individually, perhaps not. But put them together in this kind of forum and the mob rule element will come out.'

Dorothy sighed and then, sensing that Paul was itching to pick up his newspaper again, said: 'You've never really said whether you're for it or against it.'

Paul gave her rather a wintry smile and then replied: 'I don't actually see why I have to take sides. All I'll say is that if the District Council decides to put it in Motherston or Crapwell you won't find me running along to them and saying 'Please can we have it back again.'

'So you are against it, then?'

'I didn't say so. Look, let's try and be dispassionate about it. If it gets built it won't make any difference to our view from here, there'll just be a mess in the middle of the village whilst they're building it. And from what I remember about the plans and photographs they showed at the Open Day, the design of the houses or flats or whatever they are looks quite reasonable. In fact I remember some girl with red hair lobbying me about how one of the guiding principles of the Housing Association was that the appearance of what they build must never give an obvious message that it's social housing. Some of their other houses looked perfectly acceptable; you and I have both seen much uglier houses which have been built privately.'

'So what do you think Charles and the others are getting so worked up about, then?'

'Well, clearly, some people – like your friend Mr Thomas – will be directly affected. Privately, I don't have a great deal of sympathy for him. He must have been able to see that the Church Field site wouldn't stay vacant for ever when he bought his place.'

'It would be difficult for them. His wife isn't well.'

Paul chose not to pursue the point.

'The next objection is likely to be that property prices in the village would be affected.'

'And would they be?'

'I doubt it. They're far too high already. Local people are being priced out. In that sense, I see it as an argument for the development, not against it.'

'Oh, look. Can't you just tell me whether you're for it or against it?'

'For goodness sake, Dorothy, I'm just running through the arguments. You asked me to say what I thought Charles and his crew were on about. I'm trying to give you an answer.'

'And have you?'

Paul took a deep breath.

'I think the central issue is who's going to live in the houses. And this is the difficult bit. They'll have to be offered to local people, because this is what's known as a rural exception site. But if there aren't enough takers, they'll have to cast their net a bit wider. The Housing Association won't be able to afford sitting with a lot of empty properties on its books. And my guess is that this is what'll happen. And that's another reason why I'd rather avoid the meeting. All it'll need is someone like Betty Henshaw, if she's still sober enough to get her words out, to wind everybody up about illegal immigrants and ex-convicts coming to live in the village and the whole thing will get thoroughly nasty and completely out of hand.'

'Hm. You might be right. But I think you're just manufacturing reasons for not going to the meeting.'

Paul smiled, knowing how well she understood his thought processes.

'Yes, fair point. But look at it like this, please. I've spent the whole of my working life dealing with public issues. I ended up getting pretty bloody disenchanted with the whole process. I know the difference between what's rational and what's expedient. I don't want to go back into that world in a silly parochial context where the level of argument will be crude beyond belief and the expedient will win hands down because it has the loudest voices and the most money. I loathe that world. I spent too long in it. I want to spend my retirement doing private things, not reliving the world of political nastiness I had to serve for all those years. Now do you see where I'm coming from?'

'Yes, I suppose so,' Dorothy said, reluctantly.

'And are you thinking of telling me where you stand on the issue?' Paul enquired, gently.

'It does seem...rather mean and unchristian to object to decent housing for people who aren't fortunate enough to be able to own their own homes, doesn't it?'

She was about to embark on another sentence beginning with the words 'Our Lord said' but decided to suppress it. Getting Paul to talk to her properly for once had been quite an achievement, and she didn't want to risk causing him to switch off again.

'You see,' Paul went on, 'why I said that I wouldn't mind it being in Crapwell instead was that what disturbs me most isn't the development itself, it's the way it's likely to divide the village and cause lots of resentment. I don't like the idea of living in an atmosphere where people have labels stuck on them.'

‘Er…?’

‘Well, you know, you’re For it, or Against it, or you’re too cowardly or lazy to say where you stand. I don’t care for that kind of thing, but I’m afraid it’s going to happen.’

Dorothy sighed again, recognising that what he said was probably going to prove correct.

‘I tell you what, though,’ Paul suggested. ‘Once you’re a bit more mobile again, let’s give a drinks party. And we’ll make sure we invite the Fors and the Againsts.’

‘Peace in Our Time in Horton Fence, you mean?’

‘That would be a bonus, wouldn’t it? But they all enjoy their drinks. And I don’t think any of them would be ill-mannered enough to berate their hosts on the subject, do you?’

Look at them all, Brian said to himself peevishly as his screen came to life. Spend a day out of the office and thirty e-mails pile up. He saw that one of them was from Pam, but chose not to go to it first. She wasn’t in when I tried to ring her last night, so this time she can wait.

Of the thirty, at least two thirds were either routine or totally unnecessary and he deleted them immediately. The rest, at a first read, varied between mildly interesting and seriously unhelpful. I can’t understand the mindset of some of the people who work down here, he thought. I ask simple and clear questions, and what do I get in return? Irrelevant waffle – and a strong suspicion that people don’t read messages properly before they reply to them.

He decided that it would be wise to resist the temptation to fire off a few sharp responses, and opened Pam’s e-mail:

Brian

As you still don’t seem to have got the message I shall have to very blunt with you. I do **NOT** want to receive any more house details, and you might like to know that I threw the last lot away unread. My priority is helping Janet with the baby; he's not sleeping or feeding properly, and she's making herself ill with worrying about him.

And even if that wasn't going on I'm **NOT** willing to uproot myself to come down there and join you. All the messages I get from you suggest either that the job's not right for you or that you're not right for it. Either way, you can forget the idea of putting this house on the market.

Pam

PS On re-reading this I realise it came out more harshly than I intended. I do hope things improve for you, but I'm sure you can understand why I'm not for moving at this stage. I know you're impetuous and you like getting on with things, but occasionally you need to be restrained a bit. Take care!

Valerie used one of the south facing bedrooms as her place of work – studio, she had decided, was too pompous a word for it. This had caused a mild degree of friction with Heather initially, as she had argued that the bedroom she had been given was smaller and darker; but she had now filled it with so many of her own possessions and drawings that any idea of moving would have horrified her. It had become her own private withdrawing room, as she liked to think of it, where she could shut the door and live in her own fantasy world. She could summon up the characters in her stories and hold conversations with them – and they were, unfailingly, so much pleasanter and more intelligent than most of the people she had to have real conversations with when she went to school.

Like her daughter, Valerie was at her happiest when working with no distractions. The early spring light was good, and she needed it for the detail which was required in her current piece of work – a small commission, from an academic not previously known to her, for some botanical drawings to accompany an article in one of the learned journals. He must have been pointed in her direction by someone else on the academic circuit, and it was always pleasing to gain work by recommendation. She liked the way he had described himself in his letter to her as having 'only low level competence' as an illustrator; and he had been admirably thorough in specifying what he wanted. She knew, to her cost, how tricky it was to handle some people who seemed incapable of being coherent about what they wanted, even when she rang them up and tried to extract clearer ideas from them. This type of conversation usually ended up with her being asked to 'do it how you think best', and more than once the results had come in for criticism. If they knew how long it took they'd see that I work at about half the minimum hourly wage – and even less than that when I have to re-do things.

Still, no problems of that type here, she told herself. It's the work I know best, and the work I like best. There are only four drawings to do, though one of them is to be in different sections, showing how the plant he is describing differs in detail from others of the same overall species. And he's allowed me enough time to do them, so I can work at my own pace. This is how I like things to be.

The telephone rang, distracting her and annoying her. She paused before picking up the receiver, forcing herself not to sound aggrieved when she answered.

'I just thought I'd give you a ring to ask how things are going,' Barbara said. 'I hope I'm not intruding.'

'It's kind of you to ring,' Valerie managed to say. 'My mother's not finding it easy. She kept going whilst my father was still alive, but now…' She broke off, aware that her voice was starting to become shaky.

'And Heather?' Barbara enquired, cautiously.

'No better. But no worse either.'

'I see. I'm sorry you're having a difficult time. I'm here if you ever want any help.'

'That's good of you. But I think we're going to have to find a way through this ourselves.'

'Oh, and one more thing. Charles asked me to enquire whether you're thinking of going to his meeting about the housing development? He wants it to be well attended.'

'I don't know anything about it. When is it?'

'This Friday evening.'

'Ah,' Valerie replied, sounding relieved. 'In that case, no. For once Simon's got a few days off, so we're going away for the weekend. It'll be good for Heather to get away, too.'

'Yes, I'm sure you're right. Forgive me for asking.'

'Just a thought, though. If we're away and the rest of you are going to this meeting, it'll be a bit of an open invitation to the local burglars, won't it?'

'Mm, good point. Between you and me, I think the whole thing could backfire, but it's no good my telling Charles that. You've just given me another string for my bow.'

'Turnout's better than I was expecting,' Charles said to Mr Thomas, as even more people pushed their way into the Village Hall and tried to get close to the coffee table. The two of them had taken up position at the front of the room; Mr Thomas had volunteered so forcefully to take minutes that Charles had had to accept him as his right hand man for the evening.

'If it matters to people they'll come along,' Mr Thomas observed, with quiet satisfaction. 'Even on a cold wet evening.'

'Can't see any members of the Parish Council.'

'Jack Lindsay's here somewhere.'

'He's the only one with any sense. But tell me,' Charles lowered his voice, 'who are those people by the window? That big man wearing a red sweater, I'm sure I've never seen him before.'

'Ah yes,' Mr Thomas replied, sounding even more satisfied, 'I was hoping he'd come along. He's called Vernon

Sinclair. Property man. He's the one who bought Five Acres last year.'

'Weekender?'

'Probably going to live here permanently when he's finished extending the property.'

'I don't know the person he's talking to, either,' Charles said.

'Wallace. Barrister. Definitely a weekender.'

'You've done well, getting hold of all these people.'

'They've invested in the village. They're entitled to a say in what happens here.'

Charles wandered off into the crowd of people drinking their coffee, aware that he would prefer to chat with a more comfortable ally.

'Evening, Edward. Thank you for coming along. Looks like we could have a lively meeting.'

'Might be livelier than you think.'

'Eh?'

'Someone's told Laura about it. I believe she's coming along.'

'Oh.' Charles could never remember which of Edward's many daughters was which, but he felt inhibited from saying so. 'It's time to get going, don't you think?'

'You're in the chair,' Edward said, grinning.

Charles felt a touch at his sleeve, and turned to hear Mr Thomas saying: 'The Gazette's turned up. I thought you ought to know.'

'Ah. No harm in that. Let's get the troops in order, shall we?'

Charles turned and marched back towards the table at the top of the Hall, leaving Mr Thomas following dutifully after him.

'Would you all like to take a seat,' Charles commanded, hoping that he had raised his voice sufficiently to be heard.

'If there are enough seats, that is,' he said, doing his best to turn up his personal volume knob. The people at the back of the Hall still seemed much more interested in chatting to each other.

'I think we can provide a few more seats if we're short,' he bellowed. The message seemed to have got across, as the chat level reduced and everybody's attention started to focus on not being left standing. Charles looked around the seventy or so people in the Hall, trying to take in who was there and, more particularly, who wasn't. He caught the eye of James, in the second row, and they exchanged a confident wink.

'Right,' Charles said. 'I think we're ready to begin. This is a community meeting and, as so many of you have kindly turned up, I think we can safely say that it's a meeting which the community very much wants. For anybody who doesn't know me, my name is Charles Crawford. I and my family moved to Horton Fence twelve years ago when I retired from the Army. I think this is a splendid place to live, and I can only assume that all of you feel the same way. May I also say that I'm particularly pleased to see a number of people who have moved into the village quite recently.

Our purpose tonight is to open up a debate about the proposed social housing development on the Church Field site. I expect you know that it has been given outline planning permission, and that the District Council is to take a final decision the week after next. The intention is...'

The door was pushed open noisily, and two more people came in. Charles could see that one of them was Frank, presumably back late from work and trying to join the meeting unobtrusively. The other one was a dark haired girl.

'There may be some seats at the back for latecomers,' Charles announced, not trying to conceal his annoyance at being interrupted.

'As I was saying,' he went on, 'the idea is to build no less than fourteen houses on the site. This seems to many of us to be a surprisingly large number for a village of our size. What

I suggest we do, therefore, is to contribute all the information we have about the proposal so that we can reach a view as to whether we should, as a community, make representations to the District Council before it takes its decision. Is this making sense?'

'What about the Parish Council?' someone asked. Mr Thomas strained to see who the questioner was.

'Yes, that's a good starting point,' Charles said. 'I believe we have one or two Parish Councillors present?'

'Well, I'm here. Never miss a meeting like this.'

A small ripple of laughter could be heard at the sound of Jack Lindsay's reassuringly rural style of speaking.

'And what can you tell us about the Parish Council's views, Jack?' Charles asked.

'Not a lot. I don't always see eye to eye with the rest of them, to be candid.'

'But what have they said?' Everybody could work out that this question came from Betty Henshaw.

'Not a lot,' Jack replied, to sounds of increasing mirth. 'They've asked some questions, haven't they?'

'But have they got any answers?' This was definitely a Home Counties voice, and an unfamiliar one – though Mr Thomas appeared to know who had spoken.

'So what do *you* think, Jack?' Betty Henshaw asked, beginning to sound exasperated.

'I'm not sure it's the right thing for the village,' Jack replied, enunciating his words increasingly slowly. 'But I'm not sure we should be against it, either. It's not, what do you call it, one of these black and white situations, you know.'

There was a short pause, which Charles then filled by saying: 'We appreciate your position, Jack. And thank you for coming along.'

There was another silence. Charles caught his son's eye once more, knowing that he wished to say something, and tried to indicate that he should wait a little longer.

The noise of people coughing and shifting around on their seats was beginning to rise uncomfortably when a new and carefully honed voice spoke up from near the back of the Hall: 'Good evening to you all. My name is Alastair Welford Wallace. I am a barrister...'

'And a QC,' Mr Thomas muttered, leaning towards Charles.

'I bought a property at the top of the village last year, and I hope over the next few years that I shall be able to spend less and less time in London and more and more time here. Because I am new here, and I haven't had the opportunity to become familiar with village opinions on this matter, I think I may be able to bring some objectivity to the debate and I believe, Mr Chairman, that that is what you are seeking.'

'It certainly is,' Charles said. 'Please carry on.'

'As I see it, there are three main issues on which clarity is needed. They are, of course, inextricably linked, but I think it may help for us to look at them individually. The first is the issue of housing density, the second is the justification for having so many units of social housing placed in the middle of what is still a relatively small village, and the third is the issue of who will live in the houses.

The housing density issue is the easiest to deal with. If this development is to be carried out by a Housing Association, fairly high density is unavoidable. This is because of the financial constraints under which such bodies now have to operate. In the long gone days of Margaret Thatcher' – murmurs of approval could be heard at this – 'social housing developments received grants of 100% of their construction costs. These days, government has reduced the grant levels to below 50%, as well as setting a ceiling on what level of rents can be charged, and most of the balance has to be made up by commercial borrowing. It almost makes the Iron Lady sound like a benevolent socialist, doesn't it?'

Some slightly strained laughter greeted this comment, and Mr Wallace went on: 'The key point is that, if this is to be a social housing development, fairly high density is inevitable, and it is futile to try and argue against it. We must restrict our comments as to whether the design is acceptable and, from what I have seen, this has been done carefully and to a good standard.'

'After they first came along with something pretty lousy,' Betty Henshaw commented.

'I have to say that I find the second point more difficult,' Mr Wallace stated. 'It is rare for a development on what is known as a rural exception site to contain more than eight units of housing. This is where I think we need more clarity from the District Council. Their argument appears to be that the site is available, that it can only justifiably be developed at quite high density for the reasons I have just outlined, so let's go ahead and put fourteen houses on it. Is this sound planning or is it just expediency?

The third point is equally difficult, if not more so. A rural exception site means that the opportunity to live in the houses must be offered only to people already living in the community. Does the District Council have evidence that enough such people exist and are interested? If so, I believe they should tell us. If there aren't sufficient people interested, how far afield do they then look for occupants? We must bear in mind that the Housing Association won't be in a position to carry vacant properties on its books, because of the financial constraints which I mentioned. It will have to exert pressure to ensure that the houses are tenanted so that it is receiving rent from them. This is where more clarity and more openness on the part of the District Council is called for. At present we simply don't have enough information to tell us whether this is a much needed and entirely justifiable development or whether – at the other end of the spectrum of possibilities, so to speak – it could turn out to be a piece of social engineering of the worst sort.'

'Doesn't the Housing Association know something about demand for its houses? Seems a funny sort of business to spend money putting up houses if it hasn't a clue whether anybody wants them. What sort of a strange outfit is this Housing Association if it behaves like that?'

A murmur of appreciation could be heard in response to this comment, but Mr Wallace stepped in quickly to say: 'I would caution against pointing your finger too strongly at the Housing Association. As a responsible body I'm sure it will have done its sums carefully, but it is dependent on the District Council for its information. In case anybody isn't aware of this, it's the District Council which has the statutory responsibility to maintain a register of people who are in housing need. It is they who allocate people to the housing which is available. The Housing Association is there merely as a provider or, to use the jargon, as a Registered Social Landlord.'

'I think that's a very helpful contribution,' Charles made his voice boom across the Hall. 'This is by no means the first time that a number of us in this village have been made uneasy by the actions of the District Council. Now, who else would like to come in on the discussion?'

This time he gave an encouraging look towards James, who was about to rise to his feet when Charles said: 'Hang on a minute, please. Frank wishes to say something.'

'I can't do clever speaking like what we've just heard from the back of the room, but all I know is this. Unless there's housing provided which local tradesmen like me can afford, this is going to turn into a dead village with nobody but retired people living in it. And I don't want to live in a village like that. That's all.'

'Well said, Frank,' Jack Lindsay called out.

'I'd like to support that.' Another voice joined the debate. 'I am the Deputy Head of a local school. I know how difficult it is for us to attract good teachers to work in this area because of the high property prices. That's why the Government has classified people like me and nurses as Key Workers, though I can tell you that it's not a label I relish particularly. If there are to be houses available for people to buy on a shared ownership basis, where they can progressively acquire the remainder of the equity, then I would say from my viewpoint that this is something to be welcomed.'

This provoked a few murmurs of approval, during which Charles leant across and whispered: 'Who's that?'

'My neighbour,' Mr Thomas replied, sourly.

'Now then, James,' his father said, turning to him. 'I'll allow you your say.' James stood up and began by saying: 'I'll try to get to the point quickly,' only to find himself interrupted by his father commanding: 'I think you'd better come and stand out here at the front, so that everybody can hear you.'

James Crawford had inherited neither his father's large frame nor his large voice. He was a slender, fair-haired man who tended to stoop a bit because of his height, and initially he sounded diffident.

'I am James Crawford,' he said, almost apologetically. 'I work in the City, but I try to get down here as often as I can. I love seeing my parents, and I love this place every bit as much as they do.

What I've heard tonight suggests to me that this is all really about money. The District Council has the benefit of a site which it can offer for free to the Housing Association, everybody knows there's a housing shortage, so let's go ahead and build on it. And if we can't find enough local people to take the houses, we'll round up some others from Crapwell or wherever to take them so we get full occupancy. The money's driving it, rather than making sure that the right thing's in the right place for the right people. And I know there are plenty of you here tonight who aren't convinced that this is the right sort of development for Horton Fence.

What I'm saying is that the whole thing's skewed, so I want to make an offer to get it unskewed. My partners and I have had a very successful year. I expect you'll all have read about City bonuses and yes, they are big. Obscenely big, some of you might think. But it's all a question of what you do with what you've earned, isn't it? None of us wants to blow it on ridiculously expensive dinners or yachts or things of that sort. Frankly, we're too busy making money to have time to spend it on enjoying luxuries like that.'

A distinctly rustic voice could be heard asking: 'How's he able to make all that money at his age?'

'I won't try to answer that,' James said, his voice strengthening. 'I think you'd find it all a bit technical. But it's all made absolutely honestly. And we work bloody hard to make it. That's why most of us get burned out by the time we get to forty.

Anyway, my partners and I want to make Horton Fence an offer. We'll buy the site back from the District Council at full market value so that it can continue as the valued open space it's always been. The Council gets some funds it wasn't expecting, which it can use for social housing elsewhere in its territory, where the need's almost certainly greater. Everybody wins, OK?'

For half a minute there was a stunned silence in the Hall before it was broken by the unmistakeable tones of Betty Henshaw exclaiming somewhat unsteadily: 'Well spoken, young man. Whoever said the young are only out for what they can get for themselves? Ladies and gentlemen, let's all give him a big round of applause.'

Which, after a muted start, they did, some of them cheering as they did so.

Charles beamed at the gathering, trying to clap more loudly than anybody. As the noise eventually started to die down Charles was about to get up and shake his son by the hand when another voice made itself heard from the back.

'Well, if you all like listening to young people so much, you can listen to what I have to say as well. And I'll come and stand at the front too, even though you haven't invited me to do so yet.'

Many heads turned sharply to the right as the dark haired girl strode to the front of the room. She was wearing a tight-fitting plum-red sweater and black trousers. The long pendant which she wore round her neck rose and fell and occasionally glittered in the light, as if to emphasise the animated gestures she made as she spoke.

'My parents live in this village too. They have a large house, which I love to visit. I know I'm very privileged to be able to do so. But this must never be allowed to become a village where only the privileged can afford to live. The gentleman over there was quite right when he spoke about the danger of local tradesmen being priced out. And you've heard about the problems which teachers face.

As for all you retired military people, what about our servicemen coming back from Iraq and Afghanistan with serious injuries? Many of them will never be able to earn a proper living again. Are we to tell them that they're not allowed to live in a pleasant place like this? Or what' – suddenly she swung round to face Charles for a moment – 'about the young mother with two small children who finds herself on her own because her husband's run off with some other woman who gives him sex more often? Do you want to deny her the chance to do her best for her children?

I believe that every decent person is entitled to decent housing… And if you think of yourselves as decent people' – she paused, looking round the room as if to challenge people to make eye contact with her – 'you should be trying to find ways of helping projects like this, not trying to find ways of blocking them.

So' – she glared at James Crawford – 'have nothing to do

with the sanctimonious crap you've just heard. You should be ashamed of yourselves for applauding it.'

There was an awkward silence. Neither the girl, nor Charles, nor anyone else seemed to know what to do next. Then into the silence came the voice of Jack Lindsay, sounding as relaxed and unruffled as ever: 'You've spoken very well, young lady. We needed to hear that. But I imagine you might take offence if we also applauded you.'

This provoked a round of nervous laughter. The girl herself appeared unsure how to respond. Then she raised her hand, as though asking for silence, before using it to push her hair back. She smiled, a little uncertainly, before saying – in a much quieter voice: 'There's no need to applaud me. I just want you to remember what I've said.'

'I don't think we'll forget,' Charles said, heavily.

Forty minutes later Charles and Barbara were sitting rather disconsolately with their pre-dinner drinks when James came into the room, seeming to be completely unaffected by what had been said at the meeting.

'Who,' he asked, 'is that astonishing girl with the blazing eyes and the figure to die for?'

'Laura Jackson-Wright,' Charles replied, wearily. 'Noted loose cannon. And daughter of good friends just up the road.'

'Wow, is she passionate! I must get to know her!'

'James,' Barbara said. 'You have a wife.'

'Yes, mother, this is true. At least it's true for the moment. You might have noticed that she's found yet another excuse for not coming down with me this weekend.'

James's mobile phone rang and he hurried out of the room to answer it. 'Probably his wife,' Charles suggested. 'Just back from three hours at the hairdressers and wondering where he's left her dinner.'

'Speaking of which,' Barbara said, levering herself out of

her chair, 'I need five minutes to do the beans, then we can all have ours. What's the problem, dear? You look pained.'

'I must take this shoe off,' Charles said, bending forward with some difficulty to do so. 'Uncomfortably tight.'

'You mean the gout's coming on again. You really will have to go on the pills permanently. Or start losing some weight. Or both.'

Charles grunted, and reached for his gin.

8

'Aha!' Mrs Henshaw exclaimed, with a distinct air of triumph. 'This is just the kind of headline we wanted.'

Ken had noticed that she was frequently one of the first to appear in the village shop on the day the Gazette went on sale. Not only that, she always seemed sprightly, well turned out, and looking as though she had had nothing stronger than lime juice to drink the previous evening. However, there were those with whom he was prepared to chat, particularly about the proposed housing development, and others with whom he was not. Betty Henshaw was definitely in the second category, so when she waved the newspaper in front of him he suddenly became rather busy checking things on one of the shelves.

'Good man, that barrister. 'Social Engineering of the worst sort.' I'm glad they picked up on that. If it hadn't been for Edward's daughter sounding off we'd be home and dry by now.'

'Maybe she had a point,' Ken observed, still concentrating on his shelves.

'Naïve sentimentalism,' she pronounced and then, sensing that she was addressing an unresponsive audience, she made her way rather noisily out of the shop.

The previous afternoon Edward had come into the shop, and quite a long conversation about village matters had taken place. All that Edward was prepared to say about his daughter's intervention in the meeting had been to observe, with a chuckle, that she had started to display a remarkable talent for stirring things up at the age of six months, and he was sure she wasn't about to give up the habit. The conversation then shifted to Mrs Henshaw; Edward mentioned that it had been partly in deference to her that Charles had decided that there should be nothing other than tea and coffee served at the meeting.

'But a number of us reckon she brought a hip flask with her,' Edward had said, grinning. 'Did you notice how her coherence level sank steadily as the meeting went on?'

'She always looks bright as a button the next day.'

'Strong constitution,' Edward said. 'I wish mine was the same.'

'Leg still a problem?'

'Always will be. Far too many other bits are creaking as well. And I have to traipse all the way up to London tomorrow. I could do without that, the way I'm feeling at present.'

'I thought you'd retired?'

'I have. But I'm still a trustee of the pension fund, and I feel I ought to keep an eye on what my successors are doing with it. Plus Laura's accommodation arrangements are all over the place, and I've promised Edith I'd go see what's happening.'

'I didn't know she was up in London.'

'Doing a Masters now. Always the odd one out. You've more or less got to lock up the other three to get them to look at a book. With Laura you've got to lock the book away.'

The following week's Gazette also included a couple of items of interest to the inhabitants of Horton Fence. Mr Wallace had written to the paper berating them not just for getting his name wrong but for 'seriously misrepresenting' what he had said at the meeting. His letter concluded by observing: 'Clearly I shall have to resist the temptation of offering you any more soundbites, as you show a much stronger preference for an eye-catching headline than for accurate reporting of what I said about a sensitive local issue.'

However, as if to show that it was capable of objective factual recording, the newspaper carried an article conveying the news that the District Council had given planning approval for the construction of fourteen houses on the Church Field site at Horton Fence. Commenting on this, the Chief Executive of the Housing Association said that he was 'delighted that, after extended consultation, a way had been found to enable this important and innovative project to go ahead.'

A different local newspaper that week also carried an article of interest – but as its readership was in the East Midlands nobody in Horton Fence was aware of it:

WAS ATTACK RACIALLY MOTIVATED?

Police are trying to establish whether an attack on a man on Tuesday evening was racially motivated. The man, whom police have identified as Malcolm Preece, 34, was walking home when he was pushed to the ground by a number of youths, kicked and stabbed. His companion, a young Asian woman, was not harmed.

Mr Preece was taken to hospital but was allowed to return home later after receiving a total of 25 stitches to his face and arms. It is understood that his attackers were also of Asian origin.

Charles Crawford had always disapproved of complaining. In his view, which his subordinates usually got to know fairly quickly, it was a form of behaviour which simply indicated weakness. If you complained about something, what you were really saying was that you weren't up to doing whatever it was that you were droning on about.

Protesting, though, was a different matter altogether. That was a strong activity. It meant that you had firm views on an issue, that you were willing to state them, and that the issue was important to you. Even if protesting made you unpopular in some quarters it was an activity worth doing to show that you had principles and that you weren't afraid to let others know about them.

But at quarter past four in the morning the distinction between the two was starting to get a bit blurred. His big toe joint was throbbing uncomfortably. If he stuck it out of the bottom of the bed he soon became aware that his foot was much colder than the rest of him. But pulling it back in and having a sheet and a blanket resting on it just caused a different type of discomfort. It was not too bad having to get up and have a widdle at two in the morning, as his natural sleeping pattern soon sent him off again. But things were different after he had to get up later in the night, and the more he shifted about in the bed the more irritable he became about his problem. His standard line, when people sympathised with him about suffering from gout, was that it was merely inconvenient when you had to get your foot inside a shoe, it wasn't actually painful. And it looked worse than it really was because you had to resort to propelling yourself forward by using your heel, in order to avoid flexing your toe joints which was where the swelling was concentrated.

Who am I kidding with all this, he thought sourly. Let's face it, this *is* painful. And protesting won't get me anywhere. Barbara's right, as she usually is. If I was three stones lighter and I could survive happily on one small drink a day I wouldn't have to endure so much of this.

Charles hauled himself into a different position in the bed, not without difficulty, and allowed his thoughts to turn once more to his early encounters with Lynne Marshall, hoping that they would at least bring him some pleasant distraction.

He had had a couple of periods of being posted to Germany. Barbara had accompanied him the first time, but they had decided that it would be best for her just to come out for short visits on the second occasion. Normal family stuff; her parents were becoming frail and needing increasing amounts of attention, James and Peter needed to have a close eye kept on them as exams were approaching – and Charles, whilst professing regret at the separation, was secretly quite relieved that Barbara was taking care of everything at home.

So one evening Charles found himself in conversation with Lynne in the Officers Mess; she and a colleague had been sent out to deliver some training on something or other, but the colleague had disappeared to check something out for the following day and the room was beginning to empty. Lynne, by contrast, who had seemed a bit solemn and stodgy during the day, was clearly one for a party after work. And, somewhat to Charles's surprise, she liked drinking beer. A big girl in a tight uniform – always a turn on. Rather a heavy face, though she had wonderfully sparkling brown eyes and one of the best smiles Charles had seen in ages.

They had started off as members of a small group at the bar but all the others had either left or moved elsewhere in the room. Charles, observing the state of her glass, asked: 'May I fill you up?'

And Lynne, having handed him her glass, looked him up and down in the most blatant way before asking him: 'Do you think you could?'

All they needed was a nod to each other after that, and Charles demonstrated that he could indeed fill her up. So much so that, from their first night together, she never called him anything but Big Soldier. Which Charles liked, and encouraged. The next evening they made a much earlier exit from the Mess, and made use of the bottle of scotch Charles kept in his room. One of his best memories was of Lynne lying on her back next to him, breasts exposed and nipples pointing decisively upwards, reaching out to go to work on him with her hand almost inconveniently soon after they had rolled away from each other. She reached out with her other hand to collect her glass and said to him, with a cheerful little giggle:

'Hey, Big Soldier, this is the life, isn't it? Nice big whisky in one hand, nice big cock in the other.'

Ah, if only it had finished then, Charles said to himself, shifting his position again as some less comfortable memories began to present themselves. We'd have had half a dozen cheerful, uncomplicated shags and nothing but agreeable and often quite arousing memories afterwards. So why didn't I bow out then? I had plenty of chances to do so, and there wouldn't have been any hard feelings.

Vanity, I suppose. Enjoying her taking hold of me with such enthusiasm and skill and saying things like 'Ah, the one that reaches the parts that none of the others get to.' He felt inside his pyjamas; sad, useless, floppy old thing – even though it probably was bigger than a lot of others, and neither stamina nor control had been a problem for him. Particularly with Lynne. Just plain, uninhibited enjoyment for both of them – and where's the harm in that, if you're discreet about it?

Lynne left the army – Charles had never enquired why – but she made sure that he knew where she was living in London. And that was where the difficult bit began. She worked as a security guard, another opportunity for the tight uniform; and because of the type of work schedule she was on, he could sometimes come to see her during the day when he was back home and doing a desk job.

'So, my Big Soldier hasn't forgotten me,' was her first greeting. He rather suspected that she had had a drink or two before he arrived, but who was he to object to that. On another occasion, though, she suddenly turned sad and wistful and said to him: 'If you ever get tired of Barbara, you know I'll always be here for you. With open arms. And some other bits open as well if you're a good boy.'

At which point Charles started to feel sorry for her and, in a way, responsible for her. She wasn't just a fun-loving person, she had a genuine and generous nature. Although he never questioned her directly about it, she had said enough for him to gather that she had had a pretty unpleasant upbringing –

and yet he never heard her say an unkind word about anyone. Maybe her good nature became part of her undoing; too ready to believe the best of everybody, and yet she seemed to be getting ever lonelier – wanting much more than just half an hour of good sex from her visitors.

The last time he saw her he had gone along, he tried to convince himself, solely out of concern for her welfare. The moment she let him in he could see what was going on. The flat was in disorder, nothing had been cleaned or tidied properly, and Lynne had clearly been at the bottle for some while. Her hair looked a mess, she was wearing a loose shirt and some shabby looking track suit bottoms, which Charles immediately assumed she had reached for only when she heard her door bell ring.

'Well,' she said, 'I was beginning to think you weren't coming, Big Soldier. But since you're here at last…' She unbuttoned her shirt, showing that she was wearing nothing underneath it.

'No, just a moment,' Charles said. 'Never mind that, I've come to see how you are.'

'You can see how I am, Big Soldier,' she said, suddenly sounding completely sober. 'And there's nothing you can do about it. You had your chance, and you chose not to take it. So I'll take the decisions now.'

Lynne buttoned her shirt up again, whilst Charles made what he knew even at the time were some hopelessly ineffectual comments about wanting to help her.

'Look, Big Soldier,' she said, wearily. 'It was fun at the time. But it's over now. I've moved on. And you'd better do the same. Barbara will be wondering where you've got to.'

After which Charles agonised about whether he should confess to Barbara and whether he should enlist her help, or anyone else's, to retrieve the prospects of a decent person who was determined to be her own worst enemy. But he did nothing – partly because he had to fill in for a colleague in

Germany at short notice when the colleague had appendicitis – and, out of guilt more than anything, it was another four months before he returned to Lynne's flat.

The door was opened by a thin, pale, rather bad tempered young woman who had a small child over her shoulder. Seeing Charles's confused reaction she decided to seize the initiative: 'Not what you were expecting, eh?'

'I...'

'Another one, eh? Just look at you, with your smart suit and your rolled brolly, creeping along here for a quick shag when your wife isn't looking. And her dead in a pile of her own vomit! Doesn't it make you feel good to be a man, eh?'

'But I...'

'Listen' she said. 'Fuck off. And if you've got any guts, chop it off before you ruin anyone else's life with it.'

Edward arrived back from his trip to London looking weary and sounding more than normally grumpy. Edith knew that there was an element of standard ritual about his behaviour; give him time to unpack, light a pipe and have a glass of something, and good humour would return soon enough. On this occasion, though, she sensed that there was more than just a bit of travel fatigue to overcome. Not only that, she had to prise information out of him; usually, once he was settled, he would volunteer it and – if he was feeling good about things – his account of his doings would come embellished with all sorts of anecdotes which amused him. Sometimes they amused her, too.

'Mission accomplished?' she enquired, a little hesitantly.

'Meeting attended. Falling asleep averted, though not by much. Had to sit through a long presentation by the actuaries. How about that for excitement?'

'And Laura?'

'She blew into Sandra's for about three minutes and then blew straight out again. Assured me that she's got things sorted, but I didn't get a chance to get her to explain. Main thing was, she wanted to know if I was the one who'd told James Crawford how to get in contact with her.'

'Which you weren't?'

'No, of course not. I would never do a thing like that without her permission.'

It sounded to Edith as though there was going to be more to this story, but once again she had to work to get it – and her instinct told her to approach the subject indirectly.

'Does she see much of Sandra and Ollie?'

Edward appeared so sunk in thought that for a moment Edith felt that she might need to repeat her question.

'Mainly brief phone calls, as far as I can make out.'

Another silence.

'But this thing with James Crawford worries me,' Edward said. 'She's been on at Sandra about it, too. I've asked Sandra to try and find out whether she wants us to say anything.'

'So what's been happening?'

'As far as I can gather, he's behaving like a sex pest. But I don't want to do anything without clearing my lines with her first. She's so wound up about everything, if you or I did something she didn't like there'd be hell to pay.'

'Is there much we can do?'

'I could go and say to Charles,' Edward replied, with sudden animation, 'that if James's wife isn't giving him enough of what he wants he should take care of his thing by himself instead of going and waving it at Laura.'

'Well, that's one approach, I suppose.'

'It's the only one that occurs to me at present,' Edward said, with some savagery. 'But I'm sure when I calm down a bit I'll see that there are others. And in any case, the smart money's probably on you talking to Barbara anyway, the two of you can no doubt sort it out diplomatically. Charles is basically an honourable bloke, though we all know he isn't the brightest bulb on the Christmas tree. And he did spend his life serving his country. I suppose, on the scale of moral righteousness, that ranks higher than being a private money maker.'

Edith was pleased to see that, having delivered himself of this mixed bag of opinions, Edward finally felt relaxed enough to smile at her.

'Good afternoon, Colonel, I hope I'm not ringing at an inconvenient time.'

'No, Mr Thomas,' Charles managed to say. He had just been on the point of dropping off when the phone had jarred him back into consciousness.

'I have been looking at the possibility of asking for a judicial review.'

'A what?'

'A judicial review of the District Council's decision to grant planning permission for the housing development. If a person thinks that a public body has taken a decision which can be shown to be flawed because it hasn't followed the proper processes he can ask for a judge to review the decision. What do you think?'

'It's a new one to me. Costs money, presumably?'

'It wouldn't cripple us. And look how strongly everyone feels about it.'

'Mm.'

'Iris is very down about it.'

Just in time, Charles worked out that he was speaking about his wife.

'Yes, of course. I'm sorry.'

'Should we try it, do you think?'

'To be honest, you've caught me a bit on the hop. Except, ha ha, with a foot in the state mine's in I'm not much use at hopping right now. I'll ring a few people. I know,' Charles went on, suddenly brightening up, 'I'll ring Moira.'

To: All Managers
From: Chief Executive
Subject: Director of Development

This is to inform you that Brian Stanley has resigned from his post as Director of Development with immediate effect, and by mutual agreement.

Arrangements will be put in hand to recruit his successor shortly. Meanwhile, Robert Janes will take responsibility for development matters in the western end of our territory, and Mary-Ann Hutchings will exercise a similar role for the eastern end. Both officers will report directly to me.

9

Dorothy hauled herself to her feet and surveyed the progress she had made in weeding the rose bed. It was a lovely day in early June – blue sky and feathery clouds, and enough breeze to make gardening a pleasure. She had begun her task with enthusiasm and in good spirits but, as ever, she had underestimated the time it was going to take her to get the rose bed into an acceptably weed-free state. Her original plan had been to follow what she was doing by planting out some of the annuals which were still sitting in pots, but she could see that that would now have to wait for another day.

The main problem was the buttercups; they spread out from the original plant, putting new roots down every few inches. The roots quickly grew quite deep, as well; most inconvenient when they chose to grow from a point directly next to the central stem of a rose. Although Dorothy always wore gardening gloves she still managed to get her wrists and sometimes even her arms scratched at regular intervals. The shepherd's purse was a nuisance, too, still looking scraggly and ugly even though most of it had finished flowering.

She returned to her task, adjusting the position of her kneeler so that she could set about a different area of the bed. Another reason for its untidy appearance was that the lawn round the rose bed needed edging. She tried to resist the temptation to blame Paul for this omission. He was diligent enough to mow both their lawns regularly, though it seemed to her that he did so increasingly as a chore. If he was enthusiastic about the garden, surely he would have wanted to complete the job by using the shears? He had always been a tidy person – much better at putting things away than she often was – so how come that he was prepared to regard the job as complete when he could see all this shagginess still to be dealt with? And what was so important as to keep him indoors on a day as pleasant as this? When they had first moved here he spent much more time in the garden, and a lot of the re-shaping of the layout they had inherited had come from his ideas.

I must not allow myself to feel resentful, she told herself. That solves nothing, it just makes me feel miserable. And he does have a lot to do in sorting out his sister's estate. They were never exactly close, but I know she respected his judgment. And what sort of a life did she have? No children, and a husband who suddenly walked out on her in her forties to go and set up home with a girl from his office who must have been at least twenty years younger. All she would say was 'It's one of those things. I do have a life of my own, you know'. About as unforthcoming as Paul about her emotions, I never really had the faintest idea as to whether she liked me or disliked me. Probably neither, I was just a fact of life as her sister-in-law. She had to move to a smaller house after the break-up, and she quickly changed to teaching full time; when she retired she immediately immersed herself in CAB work. She only ever came here once, stopping off for a cup of tea on her way to visit a friend in Cornwall. My impression was that she couldn't wait to get away, and not just because she wanted to be ahead of the main weekend traffic.

Dorothy stood up again, aware that her back was beginning to get tired. That's the problem with mundane tasks like weeding; you start off full of enthusiasm, but it doesn't last. Time for a walk round the garden, to see how various other things are coming on.

She moved to another flowerbed closer to the front of the garden, seeing that several of her delphiniums needed staking to encourage them to keep on growing upright. As she was bending over to tie one of them to a stick she was surprised by a hearty sounding voice from the far side of the hedge.

'Afternoon, Dorothy,' Charles called out, in a voice loud enough to have been audible two hundred yards away. 'Garden's looking good.'

'Only from a distance, I'm afraid. The weeds are winning, as usual.'

'I'll take your word for it,' Charles announced. 'Gardens are to be enjoyed, not agonised over, you know. The more proper plants you stick in, the less chance the weeds have.'

'I wish it was as easy as that,' Dorothy said, straightening up and brushing a strand of hair away from her eyes. 'Beautiful day, isn't it?'

'Everything looks beautiful today. Everything, that is, except for That Down There.' Charles jerked his thumb angrily in the direction of the centre of the village.

'Ah...'

'Hadn't you seen? The Colditz Construction Corporation has started work at Church Field. Looks like it's going to be an even bigger eyesore than I feared.'

'Well, we knew it was coming,' Dorothy observed, a little nervously.

'Doesn't make it any pleasanter.' The bonhomie had gone completely from Charles's tone of voice. 'And I can't help but feel that if more of us had shouted more loudly at the right time we could have made it go away.'

Dorothy said nothing, knowing that Charles knew that she and Paul had not gone to his meeting.

'Ah well,' Charles said, a touch of bonhomie returning. 'Must get back. Can't see it or hear it from my place, thank goodness. Jolly nice drinks party you and Paul gave the other weekend. We both enjoyed it a lot.'

With which, he turned and began marching up the road.

What a mess I must look, Dorothy thought, looking down at her grubby gardening shirt and her mud-stained trousers. And Charles is always so smartly turned out, with his neatly pressed trousers and his well polished brogue shoes.

As she walked back towards the house she caught sight of her reflection in one of the windows; a thin, quite tall woman with straggly hair. She turned away quickly, not wanting to prolong the experience of looking at herself. A few weeks ago, intending it as a light-hearted comment, she had suggested to Paul that if she were to drop dead tomorrow he would probably spend every hour of the day with his nose in his books and that she wasn't at all sure that he would even remember to eat. But somehow the light-heartedness couldn't have come across as she intended, because Paul was clearly miffed by what she had said. His reply was to the effect that if *he* dropped dead tomorrow he imagined that she 'would spend all her time with dull, grey churchy women.' Is that how he perceives me, she wondered, attempting not to feel bitter about what he had said. Why couldn't they have had a proper laugh about the subject and then perhaps given each other a friendly hug?

Because we're not tactile people, that's why. We don't go in for hugs. Never have done. Harriet was quite into hugs as a child, but Malcolm never was. And now I've no grandchildren to hug, as they're so far away. I must have another go at persuading Paul that we should visit them this winter. Though the last few e-mails from Harriet have been decidedly ambiguous. 'It's been quite a bruising year for Justin, one way and another, but he appears to have survived it.' What was all that about, I wonder? Would they even welcome us going over there if they're having a difficult time? We've lost our son already, I can't face the thought of alienating my daughter as well. And Paul just uses that kind of thing as a reason for putting off the idea of visiting them.

She returned to her work in the rose bed, and to her train of thought about Paul's sister. Am I really right to think that her quality of life and her levels of happiness were lower than ours? Maybe I'm making an assumption there to which I have no entitlement. Yes, we're comfortably off, we live in a lovely place, we get by with remarkably few aches and pains considering we're both approaching 70, but am I happy? If someone were to ask me to give myself a happiness rating on a scale of 1 to 10 could I honestly give myself more than about 4? And all this stuff about the social housing development isn't helping, either. Paul was right, it is dividing the village. Charles clearly holds it against people, including us, if they weren't part of his campaign against it. When they all came to our drinks party it seemed to feature in every conversation I heard. Why can't they all just shut up about it? It's going to happen, so we have to accept it, there's nothing we can do now to stop it.

Oh, this won't do, Dorothy told herself. What's happened to the nice bright sunny mood I was in when I came out here after lunch? I know, I'll go in and have a cup of tea, then I'll give myself a change and make a cake for Mavis. It might cheer her up, and making it might cheer me up, too.

On her way into the house she paused for a moment to stare balefully at the kneeler, still lying at the edge of the rose bed. A metaphor for my life, perhaps?

Laura burst into the kitchen at the flat, saying: 'Ah, smells of hot food. Brilliant. I never got round to having any lunch and now I'm absolutely starving.'

She placed her books on the kitchen table and looked towards what was happening on the cooker. Seeing Julia pressing some meat balls into shape her enthusiasm suddenly cooled.

'How can you bear to eat that stuff? I thought you grew up on a farm!'

'Yes, I did. Makes you realistic. Look, I tell you what. I'll put some more pasta in the pan, if you look in the freezer bit of the fridge you'll find some prawns. Chop them up into bits, throw a few herbs over them and you can pretend they're clams and you're having a *vongole*. And for goodness sake have a glass of wine. You need to eat more and relax more. I'll swear you've been losing weight, and there was never too much of you in the first place.'

Laura accepted the glass of wine and the good humoured rebuke. Yes, there was quite a contrast between them, and it could well be getting greater. She looked at Julia in profile as she turned her attention back to her cooking; a well-built girl with thick, near blonde hair, a slightly freckly face and enormous blue eyes. She had the air of a young woman who had stepped straight out of some rustic period drama. And the personality to go with it, too – the most cheerful, unruffled person Laura could ever recall meeting. Maybe that explained why they got on so well together. And she had an enviably uncomplicated relationship; the only serious one she had ever had. She would probably be leaving after the meal to spend the evening, and no doubt the night as well, with Graham. He was all right, too.

'Oh, and that James Crawford rang again,' Julia said. 'I think I was suitably evasive about your whereabouts.'

'Oh, shit!' Laura exclaimed. 'Sorry, that wasn't very ladylike, was it.'

'Don't worry,' Julia replied, over her shoulder. 'We used to see plenty of it down on the farm, you know.'

'I've already had to change my mobile number so he can't get at me that way. I know!' Laura said, her animation levels rising again. 'If he rings again, tell him I'm in the middle of a passionate lesbian affair.'

'Not with me, I trust,' Julia said, quietly. Then, turning round and raising her glass, she said: 'Laura, I salute you. That is easily the daftest suggestion you've made all term.'

Then, seeing her confusion, she went on: 'Haven't you worked that one out yet? There are few things more calculated to arouse the randy male than the idea of two pretty women enjoying each other's bodies.'

'Oh, is that right?' Laura took a rather large gulp of wine to cover her confusion.

'I have it on good authority,' Julia said, giving Laura a smile of friendly amusement.

A vision of poor, sad, fat, sweaty Petra came to Laura, and she said: 'I had this German dyke panting after me last year. Nice person, but ugh! I can't imagine she'd have been worth a wank, even for James Crawford.'

Julia chortled, and then said: 'Come on, get to work on those prawns, will you. The pasta's almost ready, you've had two glasses of wine on an empty stomach, you'll be falling over in a minute if you don't get some food inside you.'

'I see the monkey business has started at Church Field,' Ken said, wearily.

'What did you expect?' Frank replied, picking up his newspaper.

'I suppose you're right. Seeing it all start has just got them going again.'

And it had, too. No sooner had the contractors moved on to the site and the various boards had gone up than the graffiti had begun. At first there were just meaningless daubs, something for the village youths to do to satisfy their urge to deface things.

They were soon removed, but Ken and others were right in expecting more to follow. Village opinion leaned towards the view that the perpetrators were actually a gang of youths who came in from Motherston late in the evening. Horton Fence's Neighbourhood Watch Co-ordinator did his best to persuade the Police to keep a watch on things, but he was told that they were seriously short-staffed and, as the holiday season was getting under way, their priority was to ensure that there was no trouble in the evenings at the main seaside towns.

For a while, it seemed as though the youths had tired of their sport. Then, as Ken told everyone who came into the village shop, rows of nails had been placed where cars regularly drove in. The contractors had missed them, but the District Council's Building Inspector found that both tyres on the passenger side of his car were flat when he had finished his visit and needed to get away to his next inspection.

'Why should he have to be the victim?' Ken asked. 'He's a good man.'

The following Sunday Margaret Wilson deliberately adjusted her sermon to include what she thought was a strong message about the need for tolerance and the acceptance of diversity, supporting it with every relevant New Testament reference she could find. Her congregation of 14 – average age 67 – listened respectfully, as they always did, but nobody commented to her afterwards.

Mike Tayfield, at home for the school holidays, showed Ken an article in one of his education journals pointing out the difficulties which teaching staff were having finding affordable accommodation in many parts of the country.

'And I expect the same sort of article's turning up in the nursing journals and the Police journals and probably others as well,' Ken commented, gloomily.

'It wouldn't surprise me in the slightest,' Mike replied, with a smile. 'What puzzles me is why people here are so against the new housing.'

'You're still quite new here. Maybe you haven't had time to get used to the ethos, if that's the right word.'

'Is it that? Or do some of them not have enough to do, now that they've retired?'

'Frankly,' Ken said, lowering his voice – though there was no-one else in the shop who could have heard him – 'the problem is that there are half a dozen people in this village who are just plain nasty about this kind of thing. And they're poisoning the thoughts of some of the others who have weekend homes here. I tell you, Horton Fence used to be a much pleasanter place than it is now.'

'To which the elderly protesters would no doubt say that it still would be if the Church Field development hadn't had the go-ahead.'

'If you like living in a right wing ghetto, that is.'

'Oh come on,' Mike smiled again. 'Surely it's not as bad as that?'

'You reckon?'

Two days later another conversation was taking place in a house directly opposite the building site. Simon Burlington had agreed to visit Iris Thomas, having received a message that she was 'very groggy and could hardly get her words out.'

He was met by her worried looking husband, holding up an empty medicine bottle as he let him in.

'I discovered this after I phoned the surgery.'

'What is it?' the doctor asked, curtly.

'Her sleeping tablets. She...'

'How many were there in the bottle?'

'Not more than about eight, I would say. You see she...'

'Let me see,' Simon ordered, holding out his hand. He glanced quickly at the label and then handed the bottle back, saying: 'She'd need a lot more than eight of these things before she came to any serious harm. Now, are you sure that's all that was left in the bottle?'

'Yes. I knew I'd have to get a repeat prescription next week. I make sure she has the medication she needs, you know.'

'Let me go and see how she's doing. I'll examine her on my own, if you don't mind.'

'She's coming round a bit more now, I think.'

Simon ignored him, having decided many years ago that this was the best way to deal with those whom he labelled privately 'the drearest and queerest'.

A few minutes later he returned and, seeing Mr Thomas still hovering uncertainly in his front room, motioned him to sit down.

'Yes, you're right,' he said, sounding a little more affable. 'She is coming round. No need to take her off to hospital for a pump-out. That's not a pleasant procedure, though sometimes it's needed. Tell me, has she done this kind of thing before?'

'No. Definitely not.'

'But she is depressed, yes?'

'Yes, she is.'

'Anything specific, or is it just general?'

'She lost her sister in a road accident three years ago. She's never really got over that. And the arthritis in her knees is getting worse. That's why she needs the tablets, to help her to get off to sleep.'

'I understand. Does she talk to you much about her concerns?'

'I know what they are. But there's nothing I can do to bring her sister back.'

'No, of course not. Has she ever had any counselling?'

'No.'

'You sound rather mistrustful.'

'Ignorant, perhaps. Is it a good idea?'

'It can be,' Simon said, deciding that it was worth trying to engage his interest. 'People can often find it easier to talk to someone they don't know than to someone more familiar. But it only works if they want to open up about their feelings, you can't send someone for counselling in the way I can send someone to see a consultant. I mention it because we have a counsellor attached to the practice. She works two afternoons a week, but we can call on her services more frequently if the need arises. Just ring up if she wants an appointment. But don't force her, she has to be of the mind that it might be useful for her to talk to an outside party.'

'I don't know about that. She doesn't go in for that kind of thing, you know.'

'I suggest you have a think about it, rather than making up your mind straight away,' Simon commented, rather more sharply. Here' – he reached into his bag and handed over a small leaflet – 'read this, think about it, and *then* take a decision.'

'Thank you,' Mr Thomas replied, without enthusiasm. I'll tell her you suggested it.'

'Meanwhile, make sure that she rests and that she eats and drinks normally when she feels ready for it. She should be over the effects of this by tomorrow.'

'And the tablets to help her to get to sleep?'

Simon sucked through his teeth.

'You're sure she needs them? It's not just a habit?'

'I'm sure she needs them. They relax her, so she can get comfortable in bed.'

'Very well. But you'll realise that I can't risk prescribing them in the quantities she's had up to now. You'll just have to come for repeat prescriptions more often. And I strongly recommend that you take charge of them yourself and administer one to her at bedtime. If there are razor blades or anything of that sort in the bathroom cupboard you'd better remove them, too. I'm afraid that people in her frame of mind can be very cunning about getting what they want.'

Simon took out his pad to write the prescription. As he did so he heard Mr Thomas say: 'Of course, she's also depressed because this dreadful housing development has been started. As you live in the village, doctor, you must agree that it shouldn't have been allowed to happen.'

Simon ignored him.

'I said, do you agree that it shouldn't have been allowed to happen, doctor?' Mr Thomas enquired, raising his voice a little.

Simon handed him the prescription, saying: 'I heard you the first time, Mr Thomas, and mercifully I haven't been struck by deafness yet. Now,' he continued, rising from his chair, 'I came here to attend to your wife. Any views I might have about the housing development are entirely a private matter. And if you'll excuse me, I have rather a lot of other patients to go and see.'

10

Meetings of the Association's Development Department had become rather strange events, as though everything was on hold. In one sense, everything was on hold – but the officers knew that construction was going ahead on the approved projects, and that other projects were still being worked up for approval.

After Brian Stanley's abrupt departure Robert and Mary-Ann were relieved to be able to get on with the work in their respective areas without being endlessly questioned and prodded by their erstwhile boss. They were told that, within six weeks, an appointment panel would be in place and that they, together with any outside candidates who chose to apply, would be welcome to compete for the vacant post of Director of Development. Then, just short of the six weeks and after they had both submitted their applications, they were told that the appointment panel would be deferred. Preliminary talks were taking place with another Association with a view to a possible merger, and it was thought inappropriate to make an appointment until it became clearer as to whether these talks were likely to progress. Neither of them was told the identity of the other party, and they were both left guessing as to whether what was on the cards was a merger or a take-over.

After a while the gossip level about the merger started to die down and Mary-Ann, always the more adventurous of the two, took it upon herself to ask the Head of Personnel whether it was still intended to hold the interviews.

'Could well be,' was the answer. 'In my view, they should go ahead. But I need to persuade the Chief Executive to think the same way.'

Any chance which she may have had to do so was, however, stymied by the Chief Executive going off sick with what was described as 'rather a nasty virus.' It was clearly nasty enough to keep him away from the office for quite a lot longer than had first been anticipated.

'I think I know what's the matter with him,' Mary-Ann suggested, before their meeting got under way. 'Cushionitis. He bears the imprint of the arse which sat on him most recently.'

'Almost makes you want Brian back, doesn't it?' someone else asked. 'Smack of firm government, and all that.'

'No, it doesn't,' Mary-Ann and Robert both replied. News had reached them that Brian had returned to a surprisingly lowly job with a local authority in East Anglia.

'I think he's better off with Little Tiddleswick District Council, or wherever it is. Trying to retrieve his career.'

'And his marriage.'

'Right, well enough of that. We'd better look at what's on the cards. If we've got no Director of Development and no Chief Executive the Board'll be getting even more muscular than it normally is.'

'Especially about Horton Fence,' Robert said.

'And they won't need us to tell them about the local aggro that's going on. Some of them are very well wired in to what's happening. What can we do to keep them happy, Robert? A number of them were very dubious about it, if I remember.'

'They approved it, though. They can't back out now.'

'True, but they'll want to know what we're doing to make sure it doesn't all go tits up.'

'Well, to answer your question, I've got time booked with Eddie on Thursday to look at the latest he's got about probable nominations. And I think we need to start earlier than we normally do to market the shared ownership properties. I've agreed with the main contractor that we'll contribute towards the cost of sending a private security firm round late at night from time to time. That's when the main vandalism seems to occur.'

'I think that's right. I can't see people rushing to buy if that sort of thing's going on.'

The other items on their agenda were less contentious, and they were able to deal with them without difficulty. At the end of the meeting someone said: 'Well, who needs a Director of Development when we can run meetings like this?'

Robert and Mary-Ann both smiled at this; then, as the meeting broke up, she motioned to him to stay behind, saying: 'There's something I need to tell you, but it's for your ears only. I've got the offer of a Director's job elsewhere, and unless this lot gets off the pot mighty quickly – which I can't see that they'll be able to – I'm going to be taking it. So the way's clear for you. Unless they're silly enough to go for an outsider again. Which I don't think they'll dare to do after they got it wrong last time.'

Ah, Robert thought to himself as he drove home that evening, but do I want the job? I'm beginning to be dubious about Horton Fence myself, and it's on my patch.

Turner pushed the door open and said: 'Paul Preece, you are invited to a Cock-Tool party. Come this way, please.'

Paul got up and followed obediently, not questioning the logic of the situation. Nobody does that, in dreams.

He was led into the main changing room, and automatically made his way towards the peg on which he hung his clothes when he had a bath. There was a lot of excitable noise from the further end of the changing room, but so many clothes had been hung up that he couldn't see any of the boys who were making it. He could hear what they were saying, though, and it made him eager to get undressed and join in. It didn't occur to him that it was anomalous for him to be doing so when he was a middle-aged adult and they were all boys of about fifteen or sixteen.

'Hewitt wins,' a voice exclaimed. 'His is definitely half an inch longer than Johnson's.'

'It's no good rubbing it like that, Johnson,' another voice said. 'That won't make it any longer.'

'And give me my ruler back before you spunk all over it,' said someone else.

Keen to see what was going on, Paul noticed that there was a door in the changing room wall. He went up to it, enquiring 'Cock-Tool Party?'

'Yes, through here,' he was told. He went through the door, but there were no boys on the other side of it. Instead, he was on a station platform; walking briskly, as he always did, towards the top end, where the train would come in and he would be able to get a seat in the first of the non-smoking carriages. Then he realised that he had nothing but his shirt on, and it was a fairly short one. Everybody else was dressed for the daily commute. Yes, this was unquestionably West Byfleet station, and lots of these people knew him, if only by sight, as a regular on the 8.09. He clutched himself, trying to pretend that there was nothing abnormal about his appearance.

Paul woke up with such a jump that he immediately caused Dorothy to wake up, too.

'What is it, dear? What happened?' she exclaimed, in alarm.

'Oh. Oh. Ah, that's better. Nothing. Just a rather unsettling dream, that's all.'

'What was it about?'

'Ah...no...it's gone already,' he replied, not altogether truthfully. 'Just as well, too.'

He settled back into bed, saying: 'Sorry to have woken you. Let's try and get back to sleep, shall we?'

But Dorothy didn't seem inclined to do so, for she said: 'No, I haven't been sleeping well, either. I'm really worried about Mavis, she's not getting any better. And poor Iris Thomas, too. I wish there was something I could do for her.'

Trying to keep the annoyance out of his voice Paul replied: 'There's not much you can do for anybody at ten past four in the morning. Let's stop talking and get some more rest, or we'll both wake up feeling miserable when the alarm goes.'

'Mummy,' Heather said, entering the room rather shyly as she knew that Valerie was concentrating on her work and didn't relish being interrupted, 'I've finished my story for the competition. Please will you have a look at it and tell me if you think it's worth my sending it in.'

'Yes darling, of course. As soon as I can take a break from this. Just leave it on the chair for me, will you.'

Heather did so, and withdrew. Valerie had wondered about the wisdom of letting her spend hours and hours on yet more writing, thinking that perhaps the time had come to exert a bit of pressure on her to do some socialising; after all, she had made one or two friends at school. Then she decided that it was best to let her get on with what she really wanted to do. She would learn to socialise when she got away from home and went to University. And the atmosphere in the village seemed to be getting sourer and sourer; the last time a doctor had to be called to see Mrs Thomas Simon had taken precautions to ensure that the visit was made by a colleague who lived fifteen miles away. 'If that mean-spirited bigot goes on at me once more about the housing development I'll be tempted to give him an injection he'll never recover from,' he had commented, and Valerie had known that it wasn't said wholly in jest.

When Valerie picked up her daughter's script she was initially surprised by its title, thinking that Heather had developed a hitherto unsuspected taste for cheap movies:

ZARKO AND THE BLACK RAIDERS

It was springtime in the town and, once again, it was the occasion for the townspeople to pay homage to Zarko. The tradition demanded that the first of everything – except humans – should be offered. So a calf, a lamb, a piglet and a duckling, among many other gifts, were assembled at sunrise. The townspeople waited anxiously for the messenger to return from the hills where the hermit lived; it was through him, they believed, that Zarko gave a message as to whether the offerings were to be sacrificed or allowed to live. It had been a number of years since they had been commanded to make any sacrifices, but there was always tension as to what would be required of them.

The messenger returned. The animals were spared. All that the hermit had passed on was that 'Zarko commands us to protect the innocent.'

The townspeople spent the rest of the day in celebration. There were other festivals later in the year when crops and fruit were assembled in homage, but Animal Day was always the major event of the year. By dusk the celebrations had died down and people went back to their houses; apart from those who had no houses to go to, and a few others who had fallen down in the street because they had celebrated too well.

When the elders of the town next met several of them voiced their concern about the people who slept on the streets. It is not good for them, they said. It is not healthy. It is not what Zarko wishes.

Maybe they are not innocent, others said. Maybe they drink too much wine. They will learn their lesson when the cold, wet weather returns and sleeping outside isn't fun any longer.

But one of the elders, recalling some earlier messages received via the hermit, said to them: 'Zarko tells us that not all men can be rich. That not all women can be beautiful.

That some people are born cleverer than others. Not all men, or women, are strong. But that the homage of each man and woman is of equal value.'

The elders considered these messages, some of them thinking privately that it was a little inconvenient that they had been remembered at this particular point in time. By the end of the meeting they had all agreed that some simple houses should be built so that those with no roof over their heads should have shelter. The town is rich enough to afford this, they decided. And if we have to ask people to pay a little more tax, they will see that it is worth it in order to reduce the risk of disease, and robbery. People who have no houses can become jealous of those who live in comfort, and they can be tempted to commit crime. But we will make sure that the houses are only for those who really need them, because they genuinely cannot provide for themselves.

The town was, indeed, quite rich. Some of its inhabitants had their own farms, others worked on the land owned by a rich man whose castle overlooked the town. In addition to the land on which he had a fine herd of cattle he grew crops of wheat, barley and maize. He also owned much of the hilly land in which metals had been found, and other townspeople worked for him both in mining the ores and in refining them into usable material. More recently, he had bought land in another country where gold had been found, and he often spent time away from the town supervising the work of mining and processing the gold. Because he was rich he agreed to pay more tax than other people; he was respected for having done so of his own accord. He was rarely seen in the town itself, but he was no absentee landowner; his reputation was that he worked every bit as hard as those whom he employed.

Returning from one of his journeys to his gold mines he noticed the row of new houses being built as he rode through the town towards his castle.

'What on earth are they?' he asked his wife.

'They are houses for people who have no shelter,' she replied.

'And whose idea is this?' he asked, angrily.

'You'd better ask the elders. I've told you all I know.'

So, the next day, he demanded to see the elders. They explained the reasons for their decision to build the houses, and pointed out that they were sure that this was in line with the teachings of Zarko.

The rich man was shrewd enough to know not to question the wisdom of Zarko directly, so he asked: 'Are you absolutely sure that Zarko has commanded that you build these beggars' houses?'

'Sir,' the elders replied. 'It is not accurate to portray them as beggars' houses. There are widows left with young children after their husbands have died. There are people who used to work for you in the mines until they sustained injury. There are people with deformities who cannot command a proper wage. They are all our townspeople, and they deserve shelter. Besides, if they are not housed properly and given decent sanitation there is a risk that they will spread disease, and then we shall all suffer.'

'You fools!' the rich man exclaimed. 'Can't you see the mistake you're making? As soon as word of this gets out we shall be swamped with beggars from all over the country asking for housing. You're turning the town into a holiday camp for the idle! And as for your nonsense about improving sanitation, when all the rest of them flock in the health risk will be much greater! Building must be stopped, and the houses must be pulled down. Give me a year, when the profits from my gold mines start coming in, and I will offer you a better solution with much less risk.'

'With respect, sir,' the elders replied, 'it is not for you to decide this. We are elected by the townspeople to do what is best on their behalf, and to act in accordance with the teachings of Zarko.'

'And how can you be so sure that you're doing that?' the rich man asked with a sneer.

'We cannot be sure,' was the reply. 'We can only interpret the teachings of Zarko to the best of our ability. But the Black Raiders have not come to our town for years, and maybe that is a sign that we are acting in accordance with what Zarko wishes.'

The rich man stormed out of the meeting angrily and rode home, hoping for support from his wife.

'I cannot understand these people,' he said. 'They are incapable of rational argument.'

'Calm down,' she replied, alarmed by his anger. 'Have a glass of wine, and tell me what's troubling you.'

He explained what had transpired at the meeting and then, still angry, he said: 'How can they be so blinkered? They think it's Zarko who sends the rain to grow the crops, Zarko who put the metal in the hills, they probably think it's Zarko's doing whenever a woman has a baby.'

His wife chuckled, hoping that her laughter would soothe him.

'I am a man of reason, not a man of superstition. The crops grow because we live in a fertile land, and we tend them carefully. The metal is there because the hills are old and because of what happened thousands of years ago. I have not become rich because Zarko made me rich. I am rich because I work hard, and because I treat those who work for me fairly. Is this not so?'

'Well, the last bit certainly is,' his wife said, fingering the front of her garment in the hope of distracting him. He had been away a long time.

'And tell me,' the rich man enquired, not yet willing to be distracted. 'Do you really believe in this Zarko?'

'I honestly don't know,' she replied, after a pause. 'Zarko's messages come to us through the hermit in the hills.'

'Puh!' the rich man snorted. 'Idle old devil. Spends all day sitting on his bottom doing no work. The people are taken in by him like a bunch of complete idiots. They toil all the way up into the hills to bring him food and drink. And what do they get in exchange? A bunch of inane pieties which any fool could have thought up!'

'Anyway,' his wife said, 'I don't see that it matters whether I believe in Zarko or whether I don't. The town is peaceful, and prosperous. The Black Raiders haven't been seen here for years, and we know that they've done terrible damage to other towns. The festivals in celebration of Zarko are merry occasions. They bring the townspeople together. That's good enough for me.'

The rich man was not appeased, though he had no wish to antagonise his wife. She was very beautiful, and whenever he returned from his travels he brought her some jewels or other ornaments. This time he had brought her one of the first gold necklaces, telling her that she now had the first ever product from his new mine. The next ones will be better, he told her; I'm afraid this one's a bit crude, the goldsmiths aren't practised enough at their craft yet. She had received it with delight.

Later that day the rich man summoned his most trusted servant, saying to him: 'The town has gone mad in my absence, and I need to teach it a lesson. Go to the Black Raiders and tell them that I am willing to pay them to destroy the beggars' houses. Find out their price; here are 25 gold crowns which you can give them to seal the deal. But tell them that it is only the beggars' houses which are to be their target.'

The servant returned the following day, saying: 'Yes, sir, they will do it. Their price is 500 gold crowns. But they insist on being paid 200 gold crowns in advance.'

'Monstrous! I never pay anybody more than 5% as a deposit. Do I get paid for my cattle before I sell them? Go back and tell them to get on with it, or the whole deal's off.'

The servant came back and reported that he had persuaded them to accept the terms, but only by adding a further ten gold crowns of his own. He also reported, with diffidence, that he had had to agree to the job being put back for a fortnight.

'Good man,' the rich man replied, handing the servant twelve gold coins as reimbursement. 'I trust you because you share my instinct for business.'

For a short while everything returned to normal, and the rich man busied himself in supervising what was happening on his estates. Then, one day, bad news struck; his herdsman came to tell him that some of his cattle were frothing at the mouth. A messenger arrived from the port saying that one of the ships bringing home a cargo of gold had been seized by pirates. The rich man was so concerned about how he was to retrieve himself from these difficulties that he had almost overlooked that the Black Raiders were now due to fulfil their contract.

The next day the town awoke to discover the carnage which had happened during the night. The new houses, which were nearing completion, had been flattened; one of the people sleeping on the streets, who was lame, had not been able to get out of the way of the Black Raiders' horses and lay dying as a result of his injuries.

The rich man's servant found himself fending off a request for an immediate payment of the balance of 465 gold crowns. He went to see his master, knowing that there would be difficulties over the payment.

'Tell their man that 100 gold crowns is all they can have for the moment. All my cattle will have to be destroyed to curb the spread of the disease. When the second shipment of gold comes in I shall be able to pay in full. Tell me,' he continued, 'have I ever been late in paying you your wages?'

'No, sir.'

'Or anybody else's wages?'

'No, sir. Not that I know.'

'Have you ever known me fail to fulfil a contract?'

'No, sir.'

'How do my employees regard me?'

'They know that you expect them to work hard, and that you pay them for doing so. You only fail to pay when they fail to work or do not do their work to your satisfaction.'

'Good, that's what I thought, too. Go tell their man all that. This is a commercial contract. They will understand.'

But the message came back that payment in full had to be made within three days or there would be 'another visit.'

Hearing this, the rich man rushed off to the port to try to arrange forward payment for his gold shipment, telling his servant to inform the Black Raiders that they need have no fear about receiving the balance of what was owed to them.

'We are not interested in that,' he was told. 'Tell your master that he must sell his wife's jewellery. The payment date cannot be put back.'

The servant hurried home and went to see his master's wife, telling her that she was in great danger as there was a risk that the Black Raiders would return.

'You must leave immediately, before your husband returns,' he urged her. 'And take all your valuable jewels with you. I will tell him that you have received a message that your father is dying and that you must go and see him straight away before it is too late.'

She considered his advice for a minute, and then said: 'I believe you. But adjust your story if you want to keep your head on your shoulders. My father died ten years ago. Tell him it's my mother.'

When the rich man returned and received the latest message from the Black Raiders he went off immediately in search of his wife. Not finding her, he summoned his servant and was told about her mother. He cursed loudly. The servant departed and found other things to do.

That night the Black Raiders arrived again. They came straight to the castle, not riding through the town, so it was a little while the next day before anybody other than the servant, who had spent the night a couple of miles away, realised what had happened. The castle had been knocked to the ground and everything inflammable had been set alight. Those bold enough to get close were shocked to see the rich man's severed head placed on top of what was left of the castle gate.

The servant, shakily, made his way in to the town to explain to the elders why the Black Raiders had suddenly appeared again after so many years of peace. They listened to him, patiently, and then asked: 'So now you have no house, either?'

'No, sirs, I have no house.'

'Do not be too downcast. The Black Raiders seem to have made a much more thorough job of trashing your master's place than they did when they wrecked the houses we're building. Anyway, they were only partly built. It will not take long before we get them reconstructed. You may live in one of them, if you wish.'

'Zarko commands us to protect the innocent,' one of the elders intoned.

'But I am not innocent,' the servant said. 'I did my master's bidding, even though I knew that what I did was wicked.'

'Yes, but you protected somebody who was innocent. You have heeded the teachings of Zarko.'

'And my master's widow? Now she has no house either.'

'Thanks to you she still has her jewellery. She can look after herself.'

Valerie was aware that Heather had slid quietly into her room whilst she was still reading her script. When she had finished she looked up and said: 'Hey, this is a bit political, isn't it? Remind me, is this competition a local one or a national one?'

'It's a national one.'
'Well, that makes me feel a lot easier about it, darling.'
'And I still just qualify for the Under 15 section.'
'Wonderful! Go for it!'

11

'Fancy a walk round the garden before you go? I haven't seen you to talk to for weeks; or at least that's what it feels like.'

'Yes, why not,' Edith replied. She and Barbara had spent the last hour with various other ladies from the village planning the catering arrangements for the Harvest Festival supper. Barbara was finding it hard to convince herself that such a dour meeting could be a prelude to what was always a jolly occasion.

'Charles and the dog have gone off for a long walk. He tends to keep well out of the way when there are meetings like this one.'

'Yes, I recognise that syndrome.'

'And both parties could do with losing a bit of weight, before winter comes on. Then it's eat as much as you can and spend the rest of the evening stretched out in front of the fire. Farting gently, and hoping I won't notice.'

'Charles?'

'Yes, he would too, if I let him.'

'Is he still having trouble with his feet?'

'Not recently. It'll be back, though.'

'And presumably he's still out of sorts about the housing development?'

'He's out of sorts about a number of things at the moment. He always gets morose when it's the end of the cricket season. Another twelve months gone by, and all that. And he's concerned about James now that he's separated from his wife – even though he never liked her much.'

'Yes, I gathered that was coming to an end,' Edith commented, wondering what this was leading up to.

'So we're off abroad at the end of the month. We'll be

seeing Peter, in Germany, then we're driving down to Switzerland. I've always wanted to see the Swiss lakes in Autumn.'

'Should be good.'

'A change of scenery should help. And Charles has a great nostalgia for his Army days in Germany. They all do, it seems.'

'Mm.'

'Actually, Edith' – Barbara paused and placed her hand on her friend's arm – 'what I really wanted to say to you was how sorry and embarrassed I am about the way James has been behaving towards Laura.'

Yes, Edith said to herself, I thought this was what we were heading towards.

'Oh, I wouldn't worry yourself too much about that,' she replied. 'From what I gather, Laura's found a way of seeing him off. The way she did it was rather over the top, but that's Laura for you.'

Edith decided not to recount the detail of the incident, of which she had been told only part anyway, and she was sure that James wouldn't have mentioned any of it to his parents. One day, working at home in the flat, Laura had answered the phone and found herself trapped, at last, into talking directly to James. Changing her normal tactics, she put on her most agreeable manner and said yes, she'd love to accept James's invitation to dinner and she was sorry they'd not managed to talk earlier. Would he like to come to the flat to collect her at 7.30 next Wednesday?

James duly turned up, to be greeted by Laura wearing a top which hardly left anything to the imagination. As she opened the door to the main room she said: 'You'd better meet my bodyguards.'

'Bodyguards?'

'Yes, they're all here to protect my body from what you want to do with it.'

James could see that the room was full of young women.

'There are nine of them. And they're all coming to dinner, too. So I hope you've brought a minibus.'

James began to raise his hand, as if to slap Laura round the face, and then thought better of it.

'All right,' he said, angrily, as he turned to go. 'I get the message.'

'Not before time,' Laura and various of the girls called after him.

And, just to make sure that he didn't forget it, when he switched his mobile on later that evening he found himself listening to them all singing, to the tune of the well-known nursery rhyme:

'Jamie put your condom on
Jamie put your condom on
Jamie put your condom on
We'll all have sex.

Jamie take it off again
Jamie take it off again
Jamie take it off again
It's all gone soft.'

'Oh, well, I'm pleased if we can draw a line under it all,' Barbara said. 'But how are all yours doing? Not giving you problems, I hope?'

Edith paused, wondering how much she should say, before replying: 'Nothing alarming, but I'm always fretting about one or the other. There seems to be a difficult atmosphere at Caroline's these days.'

'Oh. What's to do?'

'I'm really not sure. Now her kids are all a bit older you'd think she'd be finding life easier, but it's not like that. She just seems to be getting more and more exhausted. And I can't make out whether it's just coping with three lively kids, or whether there's some tension between her and Roger. She likes having me over there, but she gets very evasive if I try to get her to open up about things. And the children tend to get ratty much more often than they used to, so I imagine they're picking something up from the atmosphere in the house.'

'And you're left wondering whether it'll all blow over, or whether you should try and intervene in some way.'

'Quite. The rest are all right. Ellie's got three inches taller and suddenly gone all curvy this summer.'

'She's a lovely child.'

'Not sure she qualifies as a child any longer. And there's none of your normal teenage sulkiness with her, she's just full of herself. Perhaps a bit too full. She brought a couple of her school friends over last month, so we had three of them racing around in their bikinis.'

And I caught Byron leering at them over a hedge when he should have been getting on with his work. Maybe Edward was right about him, and we should get someone more reliable.

'And Edward?'

'Edward's had a new lease of life. Someone who used to work for him, but didn't want to be part of the bigger outfit when Edward sold out, set up his own business – and now it's started really getting somewhere he's asked Edward to be his Chairman. He was as chuffed as anything to be asked.'

'What sort of a business is it?'

'I was afraid you were going to ask that,' Edith replied. 'Whatever it is, it does it all on line.'

'And Edward understands all that sort of thing, does he?'

'Better than I do, certainly. But Edward's there to act as a sort of mentor. Wise old head, if you know what I mean. He's not there to do the technical stuff. That's probably completely beyond anyone over forty.'

'It's a pity Charles hasn't got something like that to occupy his mind, it would be good for him. I tried to get him to stand for the Parish Council, but he wasn't having any of it.'

'Well, they're not the most endearing bunch, are they?'

Edith and Barbara had almost completed their circuit of the garden when Barbara chose to voice another of her concerns: 'I don't know what you thought about her this morning, but it seemed to me that Dorothy Preece is getting even more doleful than she normally is.'

'Yes, I know what you mean. I can't say I've ever found her an easy person to talk to.'

'No, quite. Though my memory of it is that she was much more outgoing when she first came to live in the village.'

'I don't know her as well as you do. And I think they were already here when we arrived.'

'We had them round to dinner a few weeks after they gave that drinks party,' Barbara said. 'I was hoping she might loosen up a bit with a glass or two of wine inside her, but it didn't really happen. It turns out that Paul's pretty knowledgable about military history, so he and Charles spent most of the evening on that.'

'More fun for them than for you, no doubt.'

'I did try to get her on to other subjects, but she does seem to defer to him a lot. It's curious, there doesn't appear to be any great warmth between them.'

'I don't think he goes in for warmth,' Edith said. 'Edward once described him as a bag of dry bones with a brain attached.'

Barbara chuckled. 'Poor Dorothy, living with someone like that. The sad thing is, I think there's a nice, caring person underneath the rather woeful manner.'

'Do they have any family?'

'Yes, and I think that's part of her difficulty. There's a daughter who's gone to live in Australia, and she misses seeing her and the grandchildren. And, as far as I can make out, there's a son in this country who's cut off all contact with them. And she either doesn't know why, or she doesn't want to say why. I wanted her to say more, but she looked as though she was about to burst into tears all over me, and that's not exactly what you want when you invite people to dinner, is it?'

'No, but maybe that's just what she needs.'

'Without Charles and Paul around.'

'Exactly.'

'I'll think about it. And perhaps I should go and talk to Mavis, I think she confides in her.'

'Good idea. Anyway, Barbara, I must be off. Thanks for the coffee and the chat. It's nice to have a conversation that isn't about what's going on at Church Field.'

'It's time the village started being a bit more grown up about that subject, if you ask me. It's going to happen, whether we like it or not, so let's shut up about it and get on with our lives.'

But there were others in Horton Fence who had no inclination whatever to shut up about it. Construction of the houses had by now reached first floor level, and the shape of the roadway within the development had become apparent, though the tarmac surface had yet to be laid. There were still occasional outbreaks of graffiti, but the general level of vandalism had reduced – in part because the security guards succeeded in catching some of the youths on the site one evening and dealt with them in a manner which led them to look for other targets to try to wreck.

Mr Thomas managed to draw the local MP's attention to the issue by raising it with him at one of his constituency surgeries. The MP told him, fairly brusquely, that there was nothing that could be done about stopping the development, but he did allow himself to be drawn into a debate about how best to ensure an 'appropriate' lettings policy for the units which were to be rented.

Not long after this Alastair Wallace, on one of his week-end visits, invited Charles and Barbara, Mr Thomas and various others – including Vernon Sinclair – for a drink, and conversation centred on the same topic. This was one of the main concerns which I expressed at your meeting, Mr Wallace said to Charles – who hadn't forgotten, but preferred not to be reminded about the meeting because of the way in which it had ended.

'I'm not aware that we're any nearer to getting an answer,' Mr Wallace went on. 'And although, strictly speaking, neither the District Council nor the Housing Association is under any obligation to report to us about how the properties are to be allocated, as we are merely property owners in a different part of the village, I feel that in view of the interest that the topic has aroused they should be making the effort to tell us more.'

'Maybe they don't know yet,' Barbara suggested. 'It looks as though it'll be well into next year before the houses are ready to be occupied.'

'True,' observed Mr Sinclair. 'But Alastair has a good point. The characteristics of a residential neighbourhood are determined as much by the profile of the occupiers as they are by the physical appearance and style of the buildings.'

And, having secured the attention of everybody in the room, he went on to expound at some length how various parts of London and Greater Manchester had altered in tone completely as a result of the change in profile of the people living there, causing Barbara to comment afterwards that: 'Normally, at social occasions in the village, people talk to each other. Those two seem to prefer to deliver lectures. And they appear to make the assumption that we're too dim to work these things out for ourselves.'

Charles grunted, feeling that he was losing support. He had enjoyed being away on holiday, and the change of routine had prompted him to put issues such as James's impending divorce and Horton Fence's village politics well to the back of his mind. However, they were now fully in focus again, and the discussion had given him new energy to pursue his dissatisfactions about the housing development.

Others, it seemed, were of the same mind according to the Gazette, which published a front page article with the provocative heading:

VILLAGERS ARE ANGRY ABOUT HOUSING DEVELOPMENT

'The article doesn't exactly say anything new,' Paul commented to Dorothy, 'but it'll start the tongues wagging again.'

'I wasn't aware they'd stopped,' Dorothy said, rather bitterly. 'It's one of the down sides about coming to live in a small community. I feel we're dragged in to being much closer to these sorts of things than we ever were when we lived in Surrey.'

And Harriet was only half an hour away then.

'But they do have a point,' Paul said. 'If they don't tell us anything, those with a mind to do so will start spreading all sorts of rumours about who the tenants are likely to be.'

'I thought you told me that it's a rural...something or other and...'

'Exception site. Yes, the rules say that it is specifically for local people. If they can find enough. People have the right to turn down offers of accommodation if they don't consider it suitable; the District Council can't force people to live here if they don't want to.'

'No public transport to speak of.'

'No school.'

'And next year, probably no Post Office either.'

'No wonder our worthy MP is calling the District Council's decision to go ahead with the development 'questionable.''

'Well, that was a satisfactory afternoon,' Valerie said. 'The school wouldn't have any problem about accepting Heather from the start of next term.'

'Who were you able to see?' Simon enquired.

'Mainly the Head of English, though I met one or two others as well. She was very impressed with Heather getting her prize for the short story. And I liked her a lot; there'll be much more of the right kind of stimulus for her there.'

'It won't hurt us that much to pay for the rest of her education, will it?'

'It would be worth it even if it did. But now that Mother's decided to sell up, it's all coming together rather well, don't you think?'

'And what's the latest on your mother's plans for the future?' Simon asked, sounding rather guarded.

'There are two options. Go into sheltered accommodation where she is, or...move in with us if we can arrange for her to have her own space.'

'Which isn't an option here,' Simon stated.

'If she goes into sheltered she'll just moulder. Which wouldn't be good for her.'

'Yes, I see the plan. And, actually, I rather like it. If we go and live in Old Mellort, or somewhere like that, and find ourselves a house with a separate annexe we can solve most things, can't we? Closer to Heather's new school, no further away from the surgery, and you can keep an eye on your mother.'

'And get her out and doing things.'

'Quite. And I like what I've seen of Old Mellort.'

'Can you cope with the upheaval of moving?'

Simon smiled, wryly, and replied: 'If you can, I can. You're the one who'll have to do all the hard work. On top of your own work.'

'I don't mind the last bit, at all. Just gives me an excuse to be picky about what I take on.'

'And I wouldn't mind a change of domestic scenery in the slightest. I know I've never made the effort to get involved in what goes on in the village, but from what I've seen of some of the attitudes here, Old Mellort can only be an improvement.'

'I agree. Let's just make sure that Heather's happy to buy into the idea.'

When Valerie, as a courtesy, went next door to tell Charles and Barbara that they were about to put their house on the market her news was received with a judicious mixture of regret and understanding. After she had gone, Charles's only further comment was to grunt rather more loudly than usual before saying: 'I just hope Mr Thomas doesn't take it into his head to move up the hill so he gets away from being opposite Church Field. He's a near enough neighbour already.'

'But I thought he was one of your main accomplices,' Barbara said, with a smile.

'He can do that from where he is,' Charles replied, sourly.

One morning in January Betty Henshaw, looking rather more rumpled than she normally did early on in the day, went into the village shop to collect her newspaper and saw that there were copies of a new notice displayed prominently on the main counter. They had been issued by the Housing Association in collaboration with the District Council and gave advance notice that there would be five three bedroom units for sale at Church Field, on a shared ownership basis, with an expected completion date of July. It gave a telephone number for potential buyers to contact.

As she was the only person in the shop she clearly felt no need to be inhibited in expressing her views: 'What the hell do you think you're doing promoting these wretched houses?' she exclaimed, waving one of the sheets vigorously.

Ken took a deep breath before replying, as calmly as he could: 'I am not promoting them, Mrs Henshaw.'

‘Of course you are,’ she replied. ‘The information is in your shop and you are encouraging people to pick it up and take an interest in it. I call that promoting.’

‘That is not the case. As this is the only shop in the village I was asked if I would carry the information, and I agreed to do so.’

‘Well you should have known better.’

‘Excuse me,’ Ken replied, his voice beginning to shake. ‘Brenda and I run this shop for the benefit of the community. When we are asked to display information which is likely to be of interest to members of the community or to visitors we see it as part of our role to do so.’

‘It’s none of your business to connive at bringing utter scum to live in the middle of Horton Fence,’ Betty Henshaw shouted, angrily tearing up the piece of paper she had been holding.

Ken moved quickly to protect the rest of the pile and then, for the first time in the five years since he had taken over the shop, he allowed himself to bellow with rage at one of his customers, saying: ‘How dare you try to tell me what I can do and what I can’t do in my own shop? Get out of here, you vile old bag, and don’t *ever* come back into my shop. You’re a disgrace to the village.’

Mrs Henshaw stormed out of the shop, banging the door violently, and only just managed to avoid knocking Dorothy Preece flat on her back as she was trying to come in.

12

The Easter holiday weekend in the Jackson-Wright household was normally an occasion for the whole family to get together, not least because Edith's birthday happened at the same time of the year. But this year numbers were reduced; Sandra and Ollie had gone off to the States for a holiday following some meetings which Ollie had to attend in Boston. There was some anxiety expressed as to how this was going after an e-mail arrived saying 'Toby did a big sick on the plane.' Caroline and Roger made noises to the effect that they would come over if they could 'but we know you wouldn't thank us for passing on the colds the kids have given us.' Edward offered the view that this might not be the real reason for their staying out of sight, but Edith chose to ignore him.

She and Edward agreed, however, that things might get a bit difficult with nobody to keep Laura in check – but in the event they had no need for concern. Not only did she turn up in a benign frame of mind, she maintained it virtually every day. And, unusually for her, she was willing to talk about her work; her more normal pattern was to brush questions aside, leaving Edith feeling as though her daughter regarded her as not having the capability to understand what she was studying.

Edward and Edith were treated to a long and often impassioned lecture about Trauma Recovery, and how this country was not nearly as advanced in its thinking and its commitment about the subject as the USA and other countries. Laura told them that she was working on the subject with one of her lecturers called Jonas, and how they were hoping to get funding to establish a special unit to treat trauma sufferers. Edith got a bit lost in all the talk about disassociation and about empowerment of the victim; but she registered the point about Jonas telling her that it was pointless getting angry about traumatic events happening because that would always be the case, and the most constructive thing to do was to work on ways of understanding how best to handle people who were trauma sufferers and how to put this understanding to practical use.

On the Thursday before Easter Laura and Ellie walked down to the village shop to do a few errands, and Laura insisted on going to have a look at the housing development. Virtually all the houses were now complete externally, the roadways had been properly surfaced, and fences were being constructed to provide privacy for the intended occupants.

'They look all right to me,' Laura said. 'Makes you wonder what all the fuss has been about, doesn't it?'

But Ellie remained non-committal, and soon Laura was talking about Jonas again.

'Funny name,' Ellie commented.

'He's Swedish,' Laura explained. 'And he's big and blond and hunky.'

'Ah,' said Ellie. 'Are you having sex with him?'

'Yes.'

'Is it good?'

'Yes.'

'I think about having sex a lot.'

'Well, keep it at that,' Laura replied, with a flash of her usual severity. 'You don't want to be starting on all that just yet.'

Ellie turned her nose up, not liking the turn the conversation was taking.

'And another thing,' Laura went on. 'With looks like yours you're probably going to have even more trouble than I've had. The world's full of men who'll want to have sex with you, and you'll find almost all of them completely repulsive. It's no fun having to find ways of fending them off, I can tell you.'

Ellie seemed to be temporarily subdued by this, but when Laura had gone off to see Caroline to try to find out what was really going on it was not long before she regained her composure. She found her mother in the kitchen, cursing because she now had to wear spectacles in order to read her recipe books and they kept getting steamed up.

'Laura's having sex with Jonas,' Ellie announced.

'Really, Ellie,' her mother replied, using the same severe tone of voice as Laura had done, 'I don't think you should be telling me that. Some things are private, you know.'

Ellie turned her nose up again and went off to her room and her computer. Edith, having finally got her hot cross buns into the oven, removed her apron and set off in search of her husband. He was, as ever, puffing away on his pipe and looking at share prices on the Ceefax.

'Well, how are we doing today?' she asked, a little irritably.

'Can't make sense of the market at the moment,' Edward replied. 'It's up and down faster than Clinton's trousers.'

Edith chuckled, and then asked: 'Any good typos to console you?'

'Market reports are getting a bit tidier these days,' Edward said, sounding regretful. 'But I noticed on the news summary that there's increasing disquiet about pay and conditions among lower paid workers in the pubic sector.'

'Well, would you want to be paid less than the going rate for working down there?'

'Not at my age,' Edward replied, grinning.

'Oh, and whilst we're on the subject, Ellie's just marched into the kitchen to tell me that Laura's having sex with Jonas.'

'Yes, I'd worked that out already,' Edward said, removing his pipe from his mouth.'

'You had?'

'I could tell immediately. Her skin's glowing in a way it doesn't normally do. It shows that way on some women, you know. Do you remember when I had a secretary called Wendy?'

'Vaguely.'

'She was just the same. Walked in one Monday morning and it was written all over her face that she'd had a good shag over the weekend. Anyway, you're not bothered about Laura, are you?'

'Well…'

'Look, she's twenty-three, she knows what she's doing, she's easily the brightest of the lot.'

'Not necessarily the same thing as smarter.'

'Yes, perhaps,' Edward conceded. 'But she's a lot pleasanter to have around now that she's on a nice peaceful cloud. Better than having her like Jove, sitting on a storm cloud and throwing thunderbolts at everyone.'

Laura returned later in the day, agreeing with her father that there was something amiss in her eldest sister's household. 'But,' she told him, 'all I could get out of Caroline was that Roger was having to work harder than ever because it was coming up to the end of his firm's financial year. Can't see why that should make any difference. I think they're trying to hide something.'

'You could be right,' Edward observed. 'Though he is their Chief Accountant, you know.'

'Which means he has stacks of little accountants working for him. Why can't he get them to pull their fingers out?'

'Maybe he is doing. But he has to make sure they're doing it all correctly. It would be his responsibility if something went wrong.'

'Well, something's wrong, that's all I know. Or rather, that's something I suspect.'

'Me too,' Edward said, smiling at her. 'But your mother doesn't want to know.'

'I'm sure we'll find out,' Laura said. 'Unless it all goes away.'

Edith had come into the room whilst she was saying this, and Laura chose to change the subject.

'I went to look at the dreaded housing development this morning,' she said. 'It seems to be coming on all right.'

'Yes,' Edward said, with a wry smile, 'I'm afraid it is.'

'And is everybody still ranting on about it?'

'Well, I'm not.'

'Changed your mind and seen reason, have you?'

'I'm still of the same mind as I was when I first heard about it,' Edward replied, choosing not to rise to this. 'I'm not convinced that it's the right thing for this village. It would be better suited for the sort of people who live in Crapwell.'

'Byron was telling me the other day that his mum wants to have one of the houses,' Edith remarked.

'So there you are,' Laura said. 'Evidence of genuine local need.'

'Well, one swallow and all that,' Edward replied, sounding a little irritable for the first time. 'Or, in Byron's case, one galumphing great crow.'

'So what you're saying is, you've stopped ranting but others haven't. Is that it?'

'There's no point going on trying to fight battles when they're already lost. That's how I see it. Others don't.'

'But we haven't fallen out with the Crawfords, if that's what you were wondering,' Edith said, causing Laura and her father to exchange a conspiratorial wink. 'And, on a less contentious note, I saw Dorothy Preece at the village shop yesterday with a couple of grandchildren in tow. She was looking more cheerful than I've seen her in ages.'

'I'm not surprised,' Edward observed. 'Old Bonebag can't be bringing much joy into her life.'

'Hmm,' Edith commented. 'I wonder what nickname they've got for you in the Preece household.'

Dorothy was, indeed, both looking and feeling more cheerful than she had done in a long time – and not least because the change in family circumstances had come about so suddenly. Less than two weeks previously she found herself – with some trepidation because phone calls after half past nine in the evening always raised her anxiety levels – picking up the phone to hear Harriet asking 'Did you get my e-mail?' Dorothy muttered something not very coherent, as she preferred to leave e-mails to Paul, who was out at a meeting of the Historical Society, and Harriet said 'We're coming home. Justin's got a promotion and they want him back in London soonest. Can't stop, must take the kids to school.'

When Paul arrived home she immediately badgered him into opening up the e-mails, even though all he wanted to do was to have his hot milk drink before he went to bed. The message confirmed what Harriet had said, and also asked if she and the children could come and stay with them over the Easter holidays whilst Justin sorted out somewhere for them to live in London. Paul was all for leaving it overnight and replying in the morning, but she insisted that he should sit down and reply immediately, pointing out that Harriet had sent her message the previous evening.

As a peace offering she went off to make his drink, saying that she wanted to look at his reply before he sent it. But when she saw what he was intending to write her first reaction was to want to wring his increasingly scrawny neck.

'How *can* you be so off-hand about it?' she exclaimed, her voice rising in frustration and anger. 'Harriet's our daughter. This is the best news we've had in years!'

So Paul was instructed to delete everything he had written and instead to say that that they were both thrilled to hear her news and yes, they could come and stay for as long as they liked, and did they want to be collected from the airport. Even Dorothy was relieved when the return message said 'no, thanks' to their last offer.

Although Harriet had regularly sent photographs to her parents Dorothy was unprepared for everybody's change in appearance. Partly because she had lost weight, and had her hair cut much shorter, Harriet seemed to have become taller. Matthew, whom she remembered as a chubby and cheerful toddler, was now a talkative seven year old; Hannah, by contrast, hardly said a word. She was a pale, solemn child with lifeless, straight fair hair who went everywhere clutching a distinctly ragged teddy and was often to be seen with her thumb in her mouth. It was evident to Dorothy that her daughter was trying to get her out of the habit, but she could see that Hannah was bewildered by the sudden change in everything and needed some points of familiarity and comfort. Whenever her mother frowned at her Hannah would remove her thumb from her mouth, but it usually found its way back there in a couple of minutes.

It took Matthew all of two minutes after Dorothy had loaded them and their belongings into the car to start asking questions about Grandpa's computer, and whether they were on Facebook and did they look at YouTube regularly. Harriet came to her mother's rescue by suggesting that Grandma needed to concentrate on her driving, though Dorothy's chief concern was over how Paul was going to be able to cope with all this boisterousness and endless questioning. She knew how much he valued his peace and quiet, and the thought of all this noise and energy being let loose in the house was starting to make her feel more than a bit apprehensive.

As things turned out, she had no need to be worried. Matthew was clearly an intelligent child, and it was not long before Paul had him looking at old maps and asking questions about what the various symbols stood for. The process of explaining seemed to re-animate Paul, and Dorothy started feeling a bit guilty because it was so evident that here, at last, was somebody who took a genuine interest in the things which fascinated him.

Later, after the children had been put to bed – Matthew feel asleep immediately, but Hannah became suddenly clingy and refused to be left for over half an hour – Harriet and her parents had their first opportunity to talk properly. Dorothy felt that it was an oddly stilted conversation, with Harriet being a bit guarded about their reasons for returning from Australia. 'On balance, I think it's the best decision for all of us,' was the most they could get out of her – but I suppose it's still a bit awkward for all of us, she reflected. This is the first face to face conversation we've had for nearly four years. Then, as the momentum seemed to drain further, Harriet suddenly looked at them and said: 'Yes, I know. There's an elephant in the room, isn't there. You want to know if I'm still in contact with Malcolm, don't you?'

She looked intently at both her parents, gauging their reaction. Paul nodded at her without expression; Dorothy leaned forward eagerly.

'The answer is yes, I am. He knows we've come back.'

'And?' Dorothy asked.

'And that's about it, I'm afraid.'

'And he's said nothing about contact with us?'

Harriet was silent for a few moments, as if wondering how much to disclose to them. Then she replied: 'I've tried to find out what's going on. All he'll say is that he wishes you no harm provided you carry on living your lives where you are and that you leave him to live his where he is.'

'And is that the best we get from him?' Dorothy said, unable to keep the bitterness out of her voice.

'I don't get much more myself,' Harriet commented. 'I guess I've…accepted that it would do more harm than good to try to press him.'

'What did we do wrong?' Dorothy asked, sounding more and more anguished.

'We didn't do anything wrong,' Paul said. 'The question is – why is he behaving like this?'

'We must have done something wrong!' Dorothy exclaimed.

'No, look,' Paul said, as soothingly as he could. 'You mustn't assume it's your fault. Or our fault, I should say.'

'Going and telling him it's all his fault isn't the way to bring him back, is it?' Dorothy replied, her voice rising.

'I see no excuse for the way he's behaved.'

'He's our son!

'So? He's behaved in a completely unacceptable way, and caused both of us a lot of hurt and distress. He's the one who broke the bridge between us; if he wants it mended he'll have to do the mending. And until such time as he does, I'm quite content for him to keep away.'

'That's a bit cold hearted, isn't it?' Harriet suggested.

'It's self protective,' Paul replied. 'I'm deeply angry with him because of the hurt he's caused, in particular to his mother. I don't want to be alienated from him any more than she does. Or than you do. But being angry about the situation makes it easier to cope with than being upset about it.'

The following day, when they took the children for a walk through the village, Harriet was on the point of saying that things were very much as she remembered them when they came to the Church Field site.

'Gosh, those are new!' she exclaimed.

'And haven't they caused a lot of fuss,' Dorothy said, wearily.

'Why? They look all right. A bit close together, perhaps, but...'

'It's social housing. And there are those in the village who don't want it.'

'You mean it's all for rent?'

'No, not all of it. Some of them you can buy. You know, you buy half of it and rent the rest. And later on you can buy more. Though, for some reason, you aren't allowed to buy the whole of these ones.'

'Sounds a good idea to me. I've no idea what we'll be able to afford. House prices are much lower in Australia. But then, so are salaries. I wouldn't mind if we ended up in something like this. At least, to begin with.'

'I'm afraid we don't hear much of that kind of sense in Horton Fence.'

'What's the problem? Lowers the tone?'

Dorothy sighed.

'I really don't know. Some of them are scared it'll affect the value of their own houses. Some of them simply haven't got enough to do, so they use their time stirring up bad feeling.'

Harriet looked puzzled.

'I'll give you an example. My friend Mavis, who's one of the Church Wardens, is over seventy and not in the best of health. Her husband's a bit older, and they're both finding it hard to keep going in an old house with quite a big garden. They were wondering about whether they could buy one of the houses that's for sale, so that they could stay in the village. Then other people in the village got at them and scared them off, saying they'd be rubbing shoulders with all manner of undesirables. And I'm sorry to say that one of the chief stirrers is a regular member of the Church. So now they're looking seriously at moving away, which they don't really want to do at all. See what I mean?'

Harriet looked at the worried expression on her mother's face, and then said with a smile: 'You haven't changed, have you? You take everything so personally.'

'Do I?'

'Yes, you do. Come on, break the habit of a lifetime and give me a nice big hug. Because it's lovely being back and seeing you again.'

'The local MP's agreed to come and speak at the Horton Fence opening,' Rosie said.

'Has he decided to be on our side?' Robert enquired, without enthusiasm.

'I think we can take that as read. So if we have him and our Chairman and whichever Councillor the local authority puts up, do you think that'll do?'

'Sounds like the normal set-up. I can't think of anyone else we'd want to invite.'

'OK, I'll set it all up before I leave.'

'So all we need now are some tenants. And some buyers for the shared ownership units.'

'How many have you got so far?'

'Not enough. Of either. Eddie says there's quite a lot of reluctance locally.'

'I think we've done our best to promote it. If you look at it in terms of marketing spend per unit, it's had more than its fair share already.'

'Look, I'm not querying what you've done, Rosie. It's just beginning to look like a project with a curse on it. I had Desmond Harrison on the phone yesterday because he couldn't get hold of the Chief Executive. His sister lives in the village, and he seemed to be taking delight in telling me how there's still such strong feeling about it. And how he'd voiced doubts about it when it came to the Board.'

'Did he vote for it? Or against it?'

'He went along with it. But what he told me yesterday was that he had been guided by what the Board had been told about demand, and that he was beginning to think he'd been sold a complete pup. He was really quite unpleasant about it. But then he's a lawyer.'

'You could have four more takers tomorrow, then it would all look completely different.'

'I wish. And best of luck with the new job, Rosie, if I don't see you again.'

Rosie smiled serenely, and went on her way.

Yes, Robert thought, I wouldn't mind the idea of looking forward to starting a new job, either. But then I'm not a twenty-eight year old gorgeous redhead with lovely long legs.

13

'Good morning, Colonel, I hope I'm not disturbing you too early.'

'Not at all, Mr Thomas,' Charles replied, trying to sound as though he welcomed the call. 'Big day, eh?'

'Pity it's another wet one.'

'Bad weather only puts off feeble people. That's what I always say.'

'Quite right. I can't see any of us wanting to miss the opportunity just because of a bit of rain.'

'That's the spirit.'

'In the end, we decided we'd just go for the one slogan on the placards. To show we're united, you know.'

'The one that says…er…'

'WE VOTED AGAINST IT.'

'Yes. Probably the best bet. More dignified, eh?'

'That's what we thought. Will you be carrying a placard, too? We have plenty made up.'

'Ah. That's a bit of a problem. Apparently my brother-in-law is doing the honours on behalf of the Housing Association, so it would be a bit difficult for me. I'm sure you'll understand. I'll be with you in spirit, as I'm sure you know.'

There was a pause before Mr Thomas responded, and Charles was aware of it.

'Well, that's a shame,' he said.

There was another pause, which Charles broke by saying:

'Whatever he may say in public, I believe he has reservations about it privately. I hope that gives you some comfort.'

'Not really,' Mr Thomas said, allowing the end of his friendliness to show. 'If he is, as you say, doing the honours, he's bound to hand out the party line. As it were.'

'Yes. I'm afraid I have to agree with you.'

'Well, we shall still be protesting. We know it won't change anything, but we still want to make our point.'

'Quite right,' Charles said, heartily. 'I admire you and your colleagues for all the time and energy you've put into this. Pity we lost, but we've certainly made our point, eh?'

'And where does that leave us?' Mr Thomas asked, his voice suddenly devoid of energy.

'With our pride intact!' Charles almost shouted, seeking to rally him.

'Oh.'

There was another silence, which Charles found even more difficult than the previous ones. Wanting a way out of it he asked:

'How's your wife doing?'

'Not well. This is a day she never wanted to see.'

'I'm sorry. It must be hard for her.'

'It is,' Mr Thomas said, quietly. 'It is.'

'I feel for you,' Charles said, aware that he was on difficult ground. 'The two of you deserve better than this.'

'Thank you, Colonel. Now, if you'll excuse me, I have other people to ring about today's events.'

'Of course.'

With some reluctance Edward discarded his newspaper, hauled himself out of his armchair and got ready to walk down to the centre of the village.

'Says it all, doesn't it?' he remarked to Edith, as he selected the stick he wished to use, and took an umbrella from the many in the stand. 'All this time getting it ready, and then they open it on a day when it's pouring with rain.'

'Well, they've had plenty of wet days to choose from this summer, haven't they?'

'Can't argue with that. Seems appropriate, somehow.'

As they set off down the hill it was soon apparent that

others were heading for the same destination. They noticed that Vernon Sinclair, whom they had assumed was only a weekend visitor, was among those heading towards Church Field; his demeanour suggested that he wasn't turning out just out of idle curiosity. As they approached the centre of the village they could see that there were two separate groups of people gathering. One group, looking official and generally slightly uncomfortable, was standing at the entrance to the road leading into the Church Field development. A few balloons had been strung up from a lamp-post on the pavement; they were being blown about, and were scattering drops of rain as they did so. Edith noticed, to her surprise, that Charles and Barbara were among the official party – then she recalled Barbara saying something about her brother having invited them.

'Smart move on his part, I'd say,' Edward observed. 'He'll have known what Charles has been up to. Much better to have him on the inside of the tent pissing out.'

'How elegantly you put it, dear.'

'Look!' Edward said. 'Isn't that Byron's mother over there?'

'I'd say so, yes. I'm sure she'll be glad to have one of the new houses instead of that crowded little place she was in previously.'

'Byron'll soon make it feel crowded.'

Edith chose to ignore this, as she looked to see if she could recognise anyone else in the official party. Apart from Jack Lindsay all the others seemed unfamiliar. She assumed, because many of them were wearing badges, that they were people from the Housing Association and from the District Council. A rather nervous looking girl was standing in front of the group, holding a roll of coloured tape. A couple of photographers were also hanging around, as were several bored looking children. From time to time the girl said something to the children, presumably trying to maintain their interest – but she spent more of her time glancing anxiously at her watch.

The other group, whose numbers continued to grow, had formed in the main street, and seemed to be enjoying the discomfiture of the official party. As she was part of it, Edith could hear some of the comments which were being made. She could also see that the number of people carrying placards had suddenly increased, and she decided that their plan was to start displaying them sufficiently close to the time of the official opening that there would be no opportunity for anybody to prevent their messages being seen. In the other half of the group in the street, which she assumed was formed of people who had approached from the southern part of the village, she could see Betty Henshaw and Mr Thomas both prominently thrusting out their messages of WE VOTED AGAINST IT. Clearly this was the official line, though there were one or two other, less carefully prepared, messages on display. One of them, hastily scrawled in red, said: YOU SHULD HAVE BUILT IT IN CRAPWEL.

'Higher marks for the sentiment than the spelling,' Edward commented.

'Oh, come on,' Edith replied. 'Now that they're finished, they don't look at all bad.'

The church clock chimed for 12.30. The girl with the tape looked round anxiously and then walked across to talk to one of the men in suits. Edith deduced from the gestures he was making that he was wanting to wait for another couple of minutes before starting the opening ceremony. The rain began to fall more insistently; a few members of the official party, who had come without umbrellas, tried to shelter in the porches of the front two houses. All conversation within the official group appeared to have withered away, and there was even beginning to be some slightly irritable shuffling of feet in the group on the street.

Suddenly a car horn sounded, from immediately behind

the lower end of the group in the street, and a large saloon car drew up by the edge of the pavement. A tall, balding man got out of the back seat and started to walk hurriedly towards the official group. Betty Henshaw, looking as though she would have clouted him over the head with her placard but for being at least a foot shorter than him, tried to barricade his way, shouting 'You Judas! You said you were against it.'

'He's a politician,' someone else shouted. 'What do you expect?'

'How many faces have you got?' another voice enquired.

The MP turned round, as if to answer, but before he could do so an egg thrown from the other part of the group struck him squarely between the shoulder blades. A couple of the men in suits from the official group rushed forward to protect him and propel him into the relative safety of their numbers. The MP's driver, and a fierce looking man with a moustache and short dark hair, whom Edith took to be his constituency agent, got out of the car and started urging the group in the street to stand back. The girl with the tape started to unroll it, but was quickly ordered to stop by the man who now strode to the front of the official group and began his speech, announcing: 'Good afternoon, ladies and gentlemen, my name is Desmond Harrison. I am the Vice-Chairman of the Housing Association, and it is my pleasure to welcome you to the official opening of our Church Field development. I'm sorry we couldn't have provided a pleasanter day for the occasion, but there haven't been a lot of those recently. And if it carries on raining like this you'll be glad to know that it won't be long before you can take shelter inside one of the houses, and I hope you'll be favourably impressed by the quality of the accommodation which we are providing.

As I expect many of you are aware, Church Field consists of four two bedroom houses for rent, five three bedroom houses for rent and five properties for shared ownership. I wish I was in a position to report to you that all the houses for rent are already tenanted and that all the shared ownership ones already have buyers. But I can assure you that we and our colleagues at the District Council are working hard to ensure that those units currently unspoken for will soon have tenants and buyers.

For those of you who are interested in such things, the total cost of constructing Church Field came to just under 1.85 million pounds. Of this, £830,000 was provided in the form of a grant by Central Government through our friends at the Housing Corporation; the District Council provided the land and a small financial contribution, and the remaining finance was raised by the Association through a commercial loan.

I would like to thank our architects, our quantity surveyors, our building contractors – all of whom are represented here today – and all the other professionals and advisers, including of course the Association's own staff, who have helped us bring this project to fruition. In particular, I would like to thank our colleagues at the District Council – in the first place for choosing our Association to work with on the project, and then for all their constructive co-operation as we have moved towards turning the idea into the practical reality which you see today. This is the first occasion on which we have collaborated with the District Council, and I very much hope that many other joint projects will follow in the future.

I feel that I scarcely need to remind you of the severity of the need for more good, affordable housing – particularly in our part of the country, where we suffer from a combination of below average incomes and above average house prices. Clearly we cannot solve this problem overnight, but with projects such as this one I hope you will see evidence of our commitment to addressing the issue.

May I say to the tenants and to the buyers that we are delighted to have given you the opportunity to live in a village which I know well, and in which I am sure you will enjoy living. Please take good care of your properties, and please play your part in a vibrant and supportive community.

In a moment I shall ask Councillor Jean Robertshaw to say a few words, but before I do so let me explain what will happen in the rest of this little ceremony. Our MP has kindly agreed to be with us, and will be the subsequent speaker. After that we will do the official tape cutting, and then you are invited to have some refreshments in the first house on the right and to take the opportunity, if you have not already done so, to have a look around the development. It is now my pleasure to ask Councillor Robertshaw to speak. I can't exactly say that the sun has started to shine, but at least the rain has eased up a bit for you.'

A small round of dutiful applause marked the end of Mr Harrison's speech, and Councillor Robertshaw – a small, rotund woman with glasses which she kept having to take off and wipe as she read from her notes – stepped forward. But because she was facing into the wind, and had no microphone to assist her, Edith soon gave up the struggle to hear what she was saying – and it was clear from the body language of other people in the street that they were having the same difficulty.

'Shall we go?' she suggested to Edward.

'With a bit of luck she'll be done in a minute. I wouldn't mind hearing what our worthy MP has to say.'

As she turned back towards what was going on she observed Mr Thomas quietly leaning his placard up against the front gate of his house as he went inside.

Councillor Robertshaw finished what she had to say, attracting even less applause than Mr Harrison had done, and the MP walked forward; traces of the successful eggy missile attack were still evident on the back of his suit.

'Thank you very much for inviting me,' he began, his voice carrying easily to the group in the street. 'I am pleased to be here so that I can be a target for your opinions and for other things. My own opinion is very clear; there is an urgent need for good quality affordable housing, and I applaud the Housing Association and the District Council for their initiative in designing and developing these properties.

Whereas my party does not always agree with the party in government about the way in which issues in regard to affordable housing are dealt with – frankly, there is far too much micro managing from the centre by people with no discernible track record of competence in management – we fully support the policy of putting more resources towards social housing provision. I believe in a decent and fair society, with opportunities for everyone to reach their full potential. The dice are loaded against you if you don't have a decent house as the basis for your life, and I am looking forward to having the opportunity to look inside the houses so that I can appreciate what has been provided here.

I know that there have been differences of view as to the desirability of building these houses in Horton Fence, and I know that this is something of a new chapter in the life of this very pleasant village. But I really do think that it's time to put any lingering reservations behind us. Let us welcome the tenants, and the purchasers of the Homebuy properties; I hope you will be very happy in your new homes, and I am sure you will be made to feel welcome by the community as well as by the Housing Association. Thank you again, and good luck to you all.'

This time the applause was rather more enthusiastic. Desmond Harrison moved quickly to the front of the group again and signalled to the girl with the tape. After a moment of looking bewildered she realised that her moment had finally arrived, and she began to unfurl the tape, signalling to a small and scruffy looking child to hold one end of it whilst she walked across to the other side of the group. Councillor Robertshaw and Desmond Harrison took up position next to the tape; the girl belatedly remembered that she had a pair of scissors which she had to hand to them. The photographers aimed their cameras, and the two main players in the scene did their best to look cheerful despite getting increasingly wet as photograph after photograph was taken. Then, just as Councillor Robertshaw was preparing to wield the scissors, the sound of an ambulance was heard approaching. The group in the street quickly moved back to the pavement, and the tape cutting ceremony was put on hold. The ambulance, which most people had assumed was just needing to make its way past those who had been blocking its path, pulled up directly opposite Church Field. The driver and another man quickly got out of the vehicle and hurried up towards Mr Thomas's front door, carrying a stretcher. He was there to let them in.

All attention was now concentrated on what would happen next. The scruffy child dropped his end of the tape, and the girl did her best to gather it up before it got trodden on by members of the official group.

Moments later the door of Mr Thomas's house opened again and a figure covered in blankets was carried out on the stretcher and rapidly manoeuvred into the back of the ambulance, which immediately set off, horn blaring. Edith and others heard the words 'her wrists' passing among the group.

The official group stood looking totally at a loss until someone had the presence of mind to point them firmly in the direction of the house where the buffet lunch was being held. The group on the pavement dissolved in almost complete silence. Two more placards were left next to the one which Mr Thomas had parked by his front gate.

The scruffy child succeeded in his attempts to puncture a couple of the balloons. The rain started falling again, heavily.

'Extraordinary,' Paul said, cradling his cup of tea carefully. The rain had finally stopped, and a few shafts of sunlight were appearing between the heavy grey clouds. But every tree and plant was dripping from the rain and the temperature had fallen to the point where, even in July, putting your hands round a cup of tea was a welcome way of helping to restore body heat.

Paul and Dorothy had both chosen not to go and observe the opening ceremony, but news of what had happened was not long in reaching them.

'Why did she do it?' Dorothy asked.

'Who knows,' Paul replied, quietly. 'You know her much better than I do.'

'That doesn't help,' Dorothy observed, bitterly.

'Well, I can volunteer some suggestions, if you want me to.'

'Go on, then.'

Paul took a deep breath, wondering whether it was wise of him to have offered. Then he said: 'I can see three things which were probably depressing her. Firstly, being opposite Church Field. Secondly, being in pain from arthritis the whole time. Thirdly, having an obsessional and mean minded husband. Perhaps the combination was just too much for her.'

'How very rational of you.'

'You did ask, you know.'

'But at least we know she didn't kill herself.'

'Do we?'

'Yes, we do. Mavis found out.'

'Ah. That's good.'

'She could have killed herself if she'd wanted, she must know where her arteries are. So it's a cry for help. And I'm going to see that she gets it!'

A rather similar conversation was taking place half a mile up the road.

'I feel really bad about this,' Charles said, shaking his head. 'I shouldn't have encouraged him to get so involved.'

'Ah, but did you?' Barbara asked, concerned to see how strongly he was reacting.

'Yes, I did. No question about it.'

'You provided a lead. He didn't have to follow.'

'And when I heard what was said today I don't think any of us who objected came out looking good.'

Barbara chose not to comment.

'Still, we have to live with it, don't we?'

The old dog waddled up to Charles and put his head on his knee, sensing that he needed comfort. Charles patted the dog's head in an absent minded fashion.

Barbara headed towards the kitchen, sensing that Charles had had his say. What the 'it' was that he felt he had to live with could have meant any one of half a dozen things, but she decided that it wouldn't cheer either of them up if she asked him to explain.

The atmosphere was a little lighter in the Jackson-Wright household, mainly because the news that Iris Thomas's life wasn't in danger had quickly made its way to them.

Edward stood by the window of their drawing room, puffing reflectively on his pipe and looking at the way the rain had bent the roses over. There were petals all over the lawn, and bits of branches had come off some of the trees.

'It'll be days and days before we can get the lawn cut again after all this,' he observed.

'I wouldn't worry too much,' Edith said. 'The grass doesn't grow quite so quickly at this time of year.'

'Other things do. The stuff beyond the pond's getting completely out of control. Looks like a jungle down there.'

'Something for Byron to sort out next time he comes.'

'Ah, but do I trust him to know what needs weeding and what needs leaving alone? Answer, no, I don't.'

'Maybe he'll be a changed person when he goes to live at Church Field.'

'Oink!' Edward responded, flapping his arms.

'Oh, all right. But he's never going to learn much about gardening if you don't teach him anything and he just gets to do the very basic jobs.'

'I would say that Byron is working to the limit of his competence already. And that's putting it kindly.'

'Anyway, what did you make of all that schemozzle this morning?'

Edward took another long puff at his pipe before replying: 'I'm really quite shocked by it, to be honest. I know I was quite active about the whole thing initially, but once it became a done deal I gave up concerning myself over it. Frankly, there are more important things to spend one's time and energy on.'

'Quite.'

'And to see all that venom in action. Horrifying, really.'

'Horton Fence hasn't had a good day.'

'It certainly hasn't. And it's not the kind of thing that'll be easily forgotten. The MP said all the right things, but it'll take more than a few well chosen words to calm people down.'

'I just hope the village is grown up enough not to ostracise people when they come to live there.'

'I agree. Though we've a right to expect those who come to live there to behave like decent citizens.'

'Any reason to suppose they won't?'

'That's one of the things that worries me,' Edward said. 'When all this started I thought the idea was that it should chiefly be for older people. I didn't see too many of them around the place today.'

'Well, you can't expect the old and frail to stand out in the rain on a day like this.'

'True, but how many of the old and frail have actually agreed to go and live there? Charles's brother-in-law let the cat right out of the bag when he admitted that they're still looking for takers. I'm not sure I'd have made that public if I'd been doing the speech.'

'Fair point. But there's not a lot we can do about it. And it's not as if it impacts directly on us, up here.'

'True.'

'Time for a cup of tea?'

'Yes, please. Beats looking at a soggy garden. And let's just hope Mr Thomas pays more attention to his unfortunate wife when he gets her back.'

14

Edward had arrived home from three days in London; he and Edith had considered going out for a meal, but as neither of them liked any of the pubs within a five mile radius they decided that the best option was to buy in a pizza and have a bottle of red wine with it. After what had seemed like weeks of almost continuous rain some attempt at summer was finally happening, and Edith was pleased to see that Edward had returned in quite a good mood. Although she kept her concerns to herself she was uneasy about him going off for a few days and resuming the style of life he had when he was still working. He might not be willing to see the difference in his age and his energy levels since he retired, but she was beginning to be disturbed by how much he had slowed up and by how tired he became when he had one of his occasional forays back into the world of full time work. This time he had managed to combine a meeting of the trustees of his firm's pension fund with a Board meeting of the new company which he now chaired, and he had also succeeded in arranging things so that he could stay with Sandra and Ollie without getting in the way of their hectic and disorderly style of living. Or so he had assured her before he set off; she waited to see whether it had worked out this way.

With some reservations, it had. Something had gone wrong with the intended baby sitting arrangements on the first evening, so instead of Edward taking them out there was a sudden rush to the Chinese take-away. Edward hadn't eaten a Chinese meal for years, but he was pleasantly surprised by it. On the second evening Sandra had got her act sufficiently well together to invite Laura and Jonas round for dinner; they weren't exactly on time but apart from that, Edward said, it was a good evening.

'And what's your verdict on Jonas?' Edith enquired.

'Well, he matched the description – big and blond and hunky. Must be at least ten years older than Laura. More, perhaps.'

'Yes, I'd imagined that. Is he here permanently?'

'No idea. Does anybody do anything permanently these days? As far as I can make out, they've only got funding for their project for another year.'

'Did you hear a lot about it?'

'Not a great deal. Laura seemed to want to talk about it, but he didn't; I think he thought it didn't make for a cheery conversation round the dinner table. He seemed more interested in asking questions about life in Horton Fence. Said he grew up in Gothenburg, went to university in Uppsala and spent most of the last ten years in London – so living in a small village was something completely outside his experience.'

'And Laura no doubt portrayed everyone here as a bunch of elderly right wing bigots?'

'She didn't really get the chance. Snorted a bit when Sandra started painting a picture of the perfect rural idyll, but otherwise...frankly, I still can't get used to the new Laura. All this fitting in and agreeing.'

'Makes you wonder what's come over her, doesn't it?'

'A big, blond, hunky Swede, that's what. Comes over her pretty frequently, I'd say. In fact, although nothing was said, and I can't be sure, I think she may be pregnant.'

'Ah,' Edith said, trying to adjust to the news. 'Now that bit I wasn't expecting. All that stuff she used to hand out about there being too many people on the planet already.'

'Well, as I say, nothing was announced.'

'And if he's much older, is there a wife somewhere in Sweden?'

'Pass.'

'Because if there is, and there are lots of little Ulfs and Birgits running around back home and she hasn't been told, there'll be absolute hell to pay.'

'Certainly will. When was this country last at war with Sweden? Early seventeenth century?'

'Can't remember. Still, enough of that, we're in danger of getting silly about things.'

'And what news at this end?' Edward enquired.

Edith sighed.

'Not clever, I'm afraid. I had Caroline here for most of the morning.'

'What, without any children?'

'Without any children. Come on, I think we both need another glass of wine to help with this.'

Edward hauled himself out of his chair and went in search of the wine bottle.

'Thank you,' Edith said. 'Well, I guess the good news is that we now know why they've been so evasive these last few months. The rest of it's all bad news.'

'Go on, tell me,' Edward said, heavily.

'Roger's lost his job. The auditors qualified their accounts, the Board wanted to know why, so everything had to be crawled over in detail. What he'd done wasn't technically fraudulent, but it came pretty close.'

'And what had he done?'

'I got a bit lost in the detail. As I understand it, he'd presented the figures in a way which was…shall we say… something of a distortion. But by doing so he and others became entitled to a bonus. She said he'd never been happy about going down this road, but he'd been put under extreme pressure by their Marketing Director, and in the end he'd given way – partly because he also stood to gain. But clearly he didn't do it very cleverly, and when the auditors started asking questions one of his staff blew the whistle.'

'Oh, God!' Edward exclaimed, pushing his plate away. 'What an idiot!'

Then, before Edith could respond, he asked: 'And what about Caroline? What kind of a state was she in?'

'Not good. She's obviously had it up to here with the whole thing. And she's quite bitter about it all.'

'What, with him?'

'Mm. He's got some sort of payoff, though not much. I think the Chief Exec. realised that he'd been acting under duress. From the way Caroline was talking it sounds as though she doesn't really think he deserved it.'

'She's got a point. Frankly, I've never thought that much of him. Short on charm, short on warmth. Short on brains, too; if you're going to go in for creative accounting you need to be a lot smarter than he is.'

Edward reached for the wine bottle and poured out the remainder.

'How easy do you think it will be for him to get another job?' Edith asked, sounding rather apprehensive.

'Assuming he hasn't been struck off, or whatever his professional institute does to members who misbehave, he shouldn't have a problem. If he gets asked about this incident he can just present it as a difference of policy. That's if he's got enough nous. Which I doubt, frankly.'

'Caroline says he's very depressed by it all. She said she'd come out without any of the children so that he could stay with them and start rebuilding his relationship with them. Apparently he's hardly spoken to them for weeks, and when he has it's just been to tell them off for making too much noise.'

Edward shook his head. They were both silent for a while, then he said: 'It's Caroline I'm worried about.'

'Me too. And the children, of course. Frankly, she looks nearer forty than thirty at the moment. And I'm sure she's lost even more weight since this happened.'

‘Poor Caroline,’ Edward said, quietly. ‘She doesn’t deserve this.’

‘No,’ Edith replied. ‘She doesn’t. She works so hard with those children. And now it’s all falling apart.’

‘And it’s all because she married a stupid pillock. I knew at the time that she could have done better than him, but one doesn’t like to interfere.’

‘You’re right. The question is, where does she go from here? She’s got a depressed out of work husband she doesn’t respect any longer, three young children living in an unhappy household, and no income of her own.’

‘We can help her out, if it comes to that.’

‘Yes, I told her that.’

‘And?’

‘She burst into tears and just looked totally miserable.’

‘Hurt pride, eh?’

‘Mm. And feeling trapped, I imagine. She was grateful for the offer, but…’

‘Weren’t they due to go off on holiday sometime around now?’

‘That’s another issue,’ Edith replied. ‘The answer is yes, they’ve got a week booked in North Cornwall. She wants to go, he’s saying they ought to cancel to save money.’

‘Well, he’s an arse,’ Edward said, with sudden savagery. ‘He wouldn’t save much by cancelling at this late stage, would he?’

‘That’s what she told him.’

‘Can’t she go off with the children and leave him to look for another job?’

‘Seems to me that’s the obvious solution. Only he’s sulking because he heard one of the children saying ‘Can’t we go on holiday without Daddy?’

‘Oh God, the more you tell me the worse it gets! She should just go and leave him behind to live with the consequences.’

'Calm down, Edward. I agree with you, but they're his children as well, you know.'

'And a fat lot of good he is to them, too.'

'Well, anyway,' Edith said, wanting to lower the temperature, 'I think it did her good coming over here. She knows we're on her side.'

'Yes, of course we are,' Edward said, more quietly. 'The problem with Caroline is she's too docile. Always has been. And look where it's got her.'

'Can't say that about the rest of them.'

'Makes you wonder if we were too strict with her, doesn't it?'

'Too strict?'

'Well, you know, wanting to bring up our first child with exactly the same sort of values that we grew up with.'

'Yes, I see what you mean. She was always the one who told the others off, and kept on saying that Mummy and Daddy would be angry with them if they didn't stop whatever it was they were doing.'

Edward sighed, and shook his head.

'I worry about that. I really do. All that effort in programming Caroline to be a good, obedient girl – and then we let up on the others.'

'Did we? Or were they just stronger willed characters?'

'Well, they were that all right. But maybe because we allowed them to be?'

'Oh, I don't know,' Edward said. 'You do your best for them and then you find that the one who listened really carefully to what you wanted is the one who comes off worst.'

'Well, that's what it looks like today. Who knows, it may be different next year.'

'It's a bugger, isn't it,' Edward said, reaching for his pipe. 'When do you step in, and when do you let nature take its course?'

'Oh, that's easy,' Edith replied. 'They're all intelligent

adults, so you let them run their own lives. But you let them know you're there for them if they need support.'

'Well, from what you say, Caroline knows that. Let's hope she acts on it. She'll need plenty of support to get through this mess.'

'Mr. Chairman, I would like to know the current position about the take-up of properties at Horton Fence.'

'Yes, me too. Robert?'

'Of the nine rented units, six are already tenanted. Two of the shared ownership units are occupied, two are reserved, we are continuing our efforts to market the last one.'

'Or, to put it another way, several weeks after the official opening, we are still to receive any rent or any sale proceeds from about a third of the units.'

'Yes, Chair, that is correct.'

'As I recall, we put in a rather disproportionate amount of marketing effort on this scheme. Would you like to explain to the Board why this effort has met with such a singular lack of success?'

'Well, first of all, perhaps I should remind the Board that we aren't always able to let or to sell every unit by the time new schemes are officially opened, though clearly this is always our aim. Then…'

'Mr Chairman, I find it difficult to square that statement with what we keep hearing about the desperate shortage of affordable homes in the South West.'

'Yes, me too, but I think we should allow Robert to continue his explanation.'

'Thank you, Chair. Please remember also that this is the first occasion on which we have worked with this District Council, and we rely on them to make nominations to the rented units. It would appear that they have had a number of refusals on the grounds that there is virtually no public transport in Horton Fence.'

'Predictable.'

'Yes. Go on, Robert.'

'Selling shared ownership units always takes time, and would-be purchasers are beginning to find it more difficult to secure mortgage finance. And I know the Board will be aware that there has always been some local hostility towards this scheme. I think the slow take-up is due to a mixture of all these factors.'

'Mr Chairman, may I ask what proportion of the sale price of the shared ownership units are purchasers required to produce as their initial stake?'

'50%, usually.'

'And have we considered lowering this to help us shift the units?'

'It is an option, and we may have to go down this route. But for the scheme to stay within our agreed financial parameters we don't have a great deal of scope for accepting a lower initial payment.'

'Thank you for that, Robert,' the Chairman said. 'Desmond, I think you wanted to comment?'

'Yes. I have deliberately kept out of the discussion so far because, as you know, I am very familiar with Horton Fence; I think you will be aware that my sister lives in the village. My brother-in-law had quite a high profile in voicing opposition to the scheme and this, as you can imagine, placed me in something of a delicate situation.

What has been said about hostility to the scheme is quite correct, and I can't imagine that it is about to die down. Clearly our responsibility as members of the Board is to continue to support our officers and the District Council in their endeavours to get the outstanding units rented and sold.

But I have to state my concern about the way this whole episode has been handled. As members of the Board I recall that we were not happy about the way the project was initially presented to us by the previous Director of Development. In the end we were persuaded to approve it because we were given assurances about there being strong demand, which we were in no position to second guess, and because we wanted to support the establishment of a constructive working relationship with a District Council new to us.

I have to say, though, with the benefit of hindsight, that I don't think we were wise to go along with this project. My instincts have told me all along that it was too big and likely to be too disruptive for a small community; half a dozen units would probably have worked, fourteen was too big a jump to take. And though I shall no doubt make myself unpopular in some quarters by saying this, the whole project has always smacked to me of someone – whether it is here or in the District Council or a combination of the two – being on a personal crusade to change the social balance of a community which they felt for some reason deserved this kind of treatment. This sort of thing is the thin end of a dangerous wedge; the far end of the wedge is populated by people like President Ceausescu, and we all remember what he did to his country.

So, Mr Chairman, I would like to make it clear that I will not support any further projects of this type. Our concentration should be on urban areas and the larger market towns; any further development in the villages should be only on a very small scale, with much clearer evidence of need than we were given in this instance.'

'Poor old fellow, eh?' Charles said, shaking his head. 'Doesn't even want to make the effort to get out of his basket and say hello.'

'Well, the vet was realistic, wasn't she?' Barbara commented. 'He could carry on for a while, but…'

'But when do we draw the line? Yes, I suppose she's right. It has to be our decision, not hers.'

'I'm afraid so.'

They sat in silence for a while, finishing their coffee, neither of them wanting to voice what had to be voiced. Eventually Charles said: 'He wasn't too bad when I took him out on Monday. Jumped up all right when he knew it was walk time, though I realised he was struggling and that I'd have to cut it short.'

After a pause, Barbara said: 'Poor old Bucket. The spirit's still willing, but the flesh can't cope any longer, can it?'

Charles said, mournfully: 'Perhaps I shouldn't have tried to take him so far.'

'Well, he's certainly going nowhere at the moment. I virtually had to carry him outside when I came down this morning.'

'I wonder how much pain he's in. Did the vet give you any clue?'

'Not really. I think we can draw our own conclusions, just by looking at him.'

Charles sighed again.

'I suppose we…wait and see if the medication helps him to ease up a bit. And if it doesn't, then we…have to accept that it's the end of the road.'

Barbara was silent for a few moments. Then she said, quietly:

'I think we do.' Then, seeing the look Charles gave her, she added: 'I'll take him to the vet's, if you wish.'

Charles nodded, not wishing to speak. Then, having regained his composure a bit, he said: 'I suppose it's quite a good system, really. Just press the off button when it's time to go. Makes you wonder whether we should be allowed the same option, doesn't it?'

'You're being morbid, old thing,' Barbara replied. 'And, to answer your question – no, it doesn't.'

'But would I want to spend the last years of my life incontinent and dribbling and not being able to speak properly?'

'Now you're being even more morbid,' Barbara said, more briskly. 'Come on, let's leave Bucket in peace and go and see if there are any beans to pick yet.'

‘Naught for our comfort,’ Charles said, levering himself out of his chair. ‘Summer’s been a washout. Lost the Test series to the Indians. James has messed up his marriage.’

‘It’s not all bad, old thing.’

‘I’ll take your word for it. Maybe it’s me that’s the problem.’ Too fat. Made a balls of trying to stop the housing development. Still got Lynne on my conscience.

The dog groaned, trying to haul himself out of his basket to follow them, but soon gave up the attempt.

15

Paul got up from the breakfast table, took his plate and cup into the kitchen, returned the milk and the spreadable butter to the fridge, and began the washing up. He was averse to seeing unwashed dishes piling up in the kitchen, though he tried not to comment when Dorothy allowed this to happen because she was in a hurry. Today, being on his own, he could do things the way he wanted; and he knew that he would be able to start his work in a better frame of mind having left a tidy kitchen.

Even if the weather had been more inviting he would have had no intention of doing any gardening. He had indicated rather vaguely to Dorothy, before she had left to spend a few days with Harriet and the children, that he 'might do a bit if it dried up' – but the opportunity of spending a day on his own, with no shopping to do and no other distractions, was too good to miss. He went upstairs to brush his teeth and to make the bed; on the way he noticed that one or two of the indoor plants were looking a bit dry, but he decided that they could wait until later in the day to get watered. It's all too easy to allow bits of domestic administration to get in the way of what he really wanted to spend his morning doing, he told himself. They won't die if I leave them until this afternoon.

There was a small room downstairs which Paul had turned into a study, but today he needed more space in which to lay out all the various papers and books which he wanted to examine. This meant that he had to clear the dining room table of its usual clutter of newspapers, catalogues and notices about church events; he swept them all up into one pile, observing with irritation that some of them had been allowed to lie there for more than a week, and placed them on a chair.

After this he was able to fetch all his own material and spread it out. The local History Society, which had been active throughout his time at Horton Fence, had become much more so in the past year or two. Paul was spending more of his time with the Society, too, having been invited to join the Committee which planned the programme of events for the year and lined up the speakers. A number of new members had joined, two of whom were recently retired academics; Paul was pleased that they appeared to treat him as an equal, though he made no pretence of being anything other than an interested amateur.

Members of the Society had regularly undertaken research projects, publishing summaries of the results in the Annual Review. Under the influence of the retired academics the scope of these projects had widened, and Paul had taken on the task of being one of the main researchers in what had become known as the Four Families project. His family was the Mostyns; there was evidence of them having been landowners, farmers, vicars and many other occupations. At various times they had married into one or more of the other three families whose history was being investigated by other Society members. The problem, as ever, was the incompleteness of the records – but there was enough evidence to suggest that, if the pieces could be assembled and verified, a fascinating network of connections could be put together, showing how the four families had had a major influence on the development of agriculture and trade in the region.

There was source material which could be borrowed from libraries, and other items which, because of their condition or their intrinsic value, had to be copied or transcribed; Paul's excursions in search of useful records therefore tended mainly to be exercises in gathering up anything which might possibly be relevant. They were then followed by days such as today when he had the space and the leisure to sift through it all and establish how much valid and useful information he had been able to lay hands on. But the more he worked his way into the project the more apparent it became that he needed regular discussions with the other members of the Society who were tracing the history and the activities of the three other families. It was usually not long before he found that whatever new material he had picked up also contained reference to the Price family; at one stage there had been a firm of agricultural merchants called Mostyn and Price, though the Mostyn name appeared to have faded out towards the end of the eighteenth century. Perhaps one of his priority tasks needed to be to identify all the questions he could usefully discuss with Dr Ambler, who was working on the Price family history. And it was always possible that some of what he had uncovered could be of particular interest to one of his fellow researchers.

Yes, Paul said to himself, settling to his task with relish, that should give some focus to my day. I must try to resist the temptation of reading absolutely everything, fascinating though it all is. Two whole days on my own, what a luxury; maybe I should invite Ambler here tomorrow. Then the two of us can get properly stuck into it without feeling that we're neglecting Dorothy. I know she feels a bit slighted when she brings in tea and cakes and we're so engrossed in what we're doing that we hardly notice they've arrived. She made some comment about being my wife and not my secretary after the last time he came over here.

Meanwhile, Dorothy was having a much more active morning. She had undertaken to keep the children occupied and amused whilst Harriet did the grocery shopping and then made a string of telephone calls about having items of furniture and equipment delivered. They had sold a lot of their possessions before leaving Australia, deciding that this would be a better option than shipping them back to the UK and then probably incurring storage costs; for their first few months they had lived in a furnished flat, but they had now bought a flat of their own in Morden, and it was in urgent need of being properly equipped. Dorothy was privately rather horrified that they had only been able to afford what was essentially a two bedroom flat – though there was some loft space which could possibly be turned into an extra bedroom – but she kept her opinions to herself.

Matthew was a bundle of cheerful energy – give him an audience and he'll talk all day, Harriet had said – but there was very little to be heard from Hannah. She appeared to have got past the need to suck her thumb continuously, but she still clutched the tired looking teddy; Dorothy could see that Harriet had clearly spent time with needle and thread in an attempt to hold the poor thing together, but bits of insides continued to escape through the seams. She tried, without success, to get Hannah to say what she wanted to do; in the end she accepted Matthew's advice, which was along the lines of 'if you and I play a game, Grandma, she'll come and join in.' Which she duly did; she knew how to play the game, but she said hardly a word, and showed no animation at all. After a time Dorothy started to find it disconcerting making eye contact with her; every time she did so she was met with a cold, expressionless stare. Not hostile, but not friendly either – and far too reminiscent of Malcolm for comfort.

When she raised the subject with Harriet, a little hesitantly, she got an answer to the effect that there was nothing to become concerned about. Matthew's stimulated by new people and new experiences, she was told; Hannah's bewildered by them. But we had her assessed before we left Australia, and she's developing normally enough. She just takes a long time to come out of her shell, that's all.

Dorothy was still trying to work out whether she was worrying too much or whether her daughter was worrying too little when Harriet came out with the much more interesting news that she had actually met Malcolm recently. She had to wait until the children had been put to bed before she could be told the story, but she couldn't resist passing the news on to Paul, and even failed to get annoyed with him when he showed very little interest as she couldn't yet tell him anything further.

He's still living in Leicester, Harriet told her, but he's now working for a charity that helps the Asian community. They hired him as their Office Manager, but he seems to do all sorts of other things as well; and when they found out that he knows quite a bit about how Government offices work they asked him to take charge of getting grants for their work. That's why he was in London.

'And he actually asked to see you?' Dorothy exclaimed.

'Well, you could put it like that. It came out sounding more like 'I've got to be in London so I suppose we'd better meet up now you're back.''

'And how was he looking?'

'He's not changed all that much. Still thin and rather drawn. He's got a beard now.'

'Oh.'

'No, I didn't like it much either.'

'Where's he living? Is he on his own? Is he married?'

'Hang on, mother. He didn't say much about any of that, and I got the sense that if I got too curious he'd just get up and leave.'

'Oh.' Dorothy sounded suddenly deflated.

'But he asked about Matthew and Hannah, and he sounded genuinely interested in how they're getting on. Maybe there's part of him that wants to settle down and have a family.'

'And what about this charity he's working for?'

'I think the phrase he used to describe it was that it was about helping the Asian community get a better deal out of living in Britain.'

'And improving race relations?' Dorothy enquired, cautiously.

'Not sure about that. But he must be very dedicated to it. He's been mugged and beaten up by Asian youths more than once, you know.'

'No, I didn't know!'

'He doesn't make a big thing of it. Says he thinks he's more accepted now.'

'Ah,' Dorothy sighed. 'I wish I could see him again. Did he…' her voice trailed off.

'Say anything about why he'd cut off contact? Not directly.'

There was a silence, which Harriet ended by saying: 'I did tell him that I knew you and father were very hurt by the way he'd behaved.'

'And?'

'He said he didn't want you to be hurt.'

'Me?'

'Yes, you. He seems to think very differently about Father.'

'Paul didn't want this to happen either, you know.'

'I'm sure you're right. But there's some very deep-seated resentment there. And I don't think it's going to go away in a hurry.'

'Did he…say why?'

Yes, Harriet thought, recalling the conversation. But I think it would be wise to edit it a bit.

'I think he feels that…he could never do anything right in Father's eyes. I know a lot of it's paranoia, but it's what registers with him. And I guess we're all driven by our perceptions. He says he wouldn't want to talk to Father about the work he's doing now because he knows he wouldn't approve.'

'If it's what Malcolm wants to do, Paul would be very proud of him. Deep down, he didn't get a lot of satisfaction out of being in the Civil Service. He would have preferred to have done something else with his life.'

'Oh yes, I've known that for a long time. But that's not what Malcolm sees.'

'So...?'

'So what does he see, you mean?'

Dorothy nodded.

'He sees someone who only deals in disapproval. I think the most significant thing he said was 'All the time I was growing up he never said 'Well Done.' All I heard were messages about how I ought to have done better.'

Then, seeing the doleful expression on her mother's face, Harriet said: 'Look, if we handle this carefully, we might be able to arrange it so that you're here when he has to come to London again. But we mustn't rush it.'

What Malcolm had actually said was: 'If only she had the sense to put some distance between herself and him she'd make life a lot easier. For both of us.'

But this, Harriet decided, was best edited out.

Towards the end of the summer holidays Ellie insisted on having a school friend called Josie to come and stay. Edith couldn't quite understand the urgency of the request, as they would be seeing each other again in another week's time, but she was willing to go along with it. After all, she said to Edward, we'll soon have nothing but grown-up daughters; then we really will start feeling old.

There was plenty of boisterousness on the first evening of Josie's visit, and Edward was secretly relieved that Ellie arranged for them to go and see a film with a friend. In keeping with her normal approach to life and people, Ellie had persuaded the friend to provide transport for them all.

At breakfast the next morning there were still plenty of giggles and furtive exchanges of looks – so much so that Edith began to wonder quite what had been going on in the bedroom which the two of them had been sharing. She noticed that Ellie, who usually wore a bra, had either forgotten it or deliberately chosen not to put it on. Deciding that it was time to get them to do something useful for the household, she sent them off to the village shop to collect the local paper and to buy some stamps and envelopes.

Ken had to go to search for the envelopes they wanted, in the storeroom beyond the back of the shop. Whilst he was out, Ellie decided to resume their pre-breakfast playing, adding to it by arranging her hair across her breasts and suddenly pushing it aside and blowing an extravagant kiss towards her friend. As she did so she leaned backwards, so that her nipples pushed at the fabric of her top. Josie grinned, encouraging her to go on – and ignoring the fact that there was somebody else in the shop.

But Byron, unaware of Josie's presence, took it that Ellie's gestures were made for him. He threw down the magazine he had been looking at and lunged towards Ellie, pinning her against the wall with one hand and ripping off her top with one violent yank with the other. He was on the point of ripping off her jeans as well when he heard Josie yell 'Stop!'

The noise distracted him sufficiently to allow Ellie to wriggle free from his grasp and to head for the front door of the shop, screaming hysterically and trying to cover herself. She could see that a car was driving up the road and some instinct told her to flatten herself against the outside of the shop window.

Ken, hearing the noise, rushed back into the shop, saw Byron – and Josie, now screaming and sobbing – and shouted 'Oh, not you again!' This caused Byron, all seventeen and a half stone of him, to hurtle towards the front door and out into the road. His momentum was so great that he was completely unable to avoid colliding with the car even though Betty Henshaw, who was driving it, did her best to brake and avoid him. He cannoned into the front wheel casing. The impact projected him forwards and upwards, his head crashed against the windscreen and he slithered off the far side of the bonnet of the car, coming to rest with a prodigious thud in the middle of the road.

Mike Tayfield, riding his bicycle in the opposite direction, only just managed to avoid making matters worse by cycling over Byron's prone body. He was quick to piece together what had happened; he abandoned his bicycle, gathered up Ellie and Josie and marched them rapidly into his house, only a hundred yards away.

Betty Henshaw switched off her car engine and got out. Shaken by the sudden, violent incident, she had to support herself by keeping one hand on the bonnet of the car as she gazed in bewilderment at Byron, motionless in the road, and at the dents he had made in the front of her car.

A couple of minutes later Ken came out of the shop, saying loudly – for a number of other people had heard the noise and had come to see what was happening – 'Ambulance is on its way.'

Betty Henshaw, still bewildered, said 'There was nothing I could do to avoid him.'

Ken ignored her and went to pick up Mike's bicycle and prop it against the front of the shop. Then he got down next to Byron, felt his pulse and checked his breathing. By now Byron's mother and one of his younger brothers had joined the small crowd.

The ambulance arrived with commendable promptness and was followed remarkably quickly by a police car. The driver of the ambulance and his assistant bent over Byron, still motionless in the road, and began to assess how they were going to manoeuvre his considerable bulk into their vehicle. Mike Tayfield, having summoned Edith to take the girls away, had returned to the scene of the accident. Ken deduced that he was telling Byron's mother what had happened.

'Well,' Betty Henshaw said, to nobody in particular, 'I think I'll go home now.'

'Oh no, you don't!' Ken said, his distaste for her evident in his tone of voice. 'The police will need you to make a statement.' Then, moving quickly round to the front offside door of her car, he reached in and removed the ignition key.

The policeman nodded approvingly and crossed over to them; Ken explained that the only people who had seen what had happened were Betty Henshaw, Mike Tayfield and, to a lesser extent, himself. The policeman quickly accepted that the girls would be too distressed to be asked to say anything straight away. Ken heard Byron's young brother asking: 'Will Byron be all right, Mum?'

'Byron will never be all right,' his mother replied, bitterly. 'He's just like his father was. Only worse.'

The policeman turned to Betty Henshaw and held out a breathalysing kit, saying: 'Standard procedure after an accident, Madam. Nothing to worry about, I'm sure.'

But when he took it back from her and looked at the reading his tone of voice changed and he said: 'Or perhaps there is. You do realise that it's only ten to ten in the morning, don't you, Madam?'

She glared at him, malevolently. Ken smirked. Mike tried not to look embarrassed.

'Do we know where she lives?' the policeman asked.

'In the village,' Ken replied.

'Right,' the policeman said to her, very firmly. 'There's no way I'm going to allow you to drive that car home. After the three of you have given me your statements you will go and sit in my car until I'm ready to take you home. Your car will have to be retrieved some other time.'

When he returned after depositing her back home, having told her in no uncertain fashion what would happen to her if she was seen driving again, the ambulance staff had managed to lever Byron, now groaning intermittently, on to a stretcher and were getting ready to lift him into the vehicle. The policeman gave them an enquiring look.

‘Concussed,’ one of them replied. ‘Probably a few broken ribs and maybe a broken shoulder as well. And possibly some brain damage.’

‘Can’t be,’ Byron’s mother said. ‘He hasn’t got a brain.’

The ambulance men chose to ignore this, saying: ‘His life’s not in danger. We’ll look after him.’

‘You can have him,’ she retorted. ‘Useless great git. Come on, Freddy, let’s go home. We need a good strong cup of tea.’

Five minutes later the ambulance had gone off, the policeman had made a couple of calls on his mobile phone and also departed, everybody else had resumed their morning activities and Horton Fence was as peaceful as it usually was midway through the morning – so much so that when Paul Preece came into the shop to post some books he could see no evidence of what had so recently gone on. And Ken, who regularly received village gossip but hardly ever initiated it, saw no reason for telling him the story of the morning’s events.

16

In early May of the following year the Jackson-Wrights gave another of their drinks parties. Once again they had succeeded in picking a fine day for the occasion – quite an achievement, as a number of their guests remarked, because most of the previous month had been cold and often wet. The waiters were in evidence again, leaving Edward and Edith free to chat with people. There was even an extra waiter in the form of Toby, now nearly five; he had latched on to his mother's idea of circulating among the groups of people standing on the lawn and offering a bowl of crisps to them. This worked well when they noticed he was there, but when Sandra observed him trying to attract the attention of a rather large lady by ramming the bowl of crisps into her bottom she intervened and suggested that he might prefer to go off and play with his cousins. The owner of the bottom, who turned out to be Mrs Vernon Sinclair, was not in the least offended; she seemed glad to have an opportunity to get away from listening to her husband pontificating about something to do with property so that she could talk to Sandra instead.

'Quite a special occasion,' Sandra said. 'I can't remember when all four of us were last here together.'

'Tell me who's who,' Mrs Sinclair said, sounding genuinely interested. 'We haven't got to know many people in the village yet.'

'Well, I'll start with the home team. The girl over there with the long gold hair is Ellie. She's my youngest sister.'

'Yes, I'd noticed her.'

'It's difficult not to. Ellie doesn't do melting into the background. And Laura's around somewhere. I saw her earlier, maybe she's gone off to feed the baby. That's her partner, talking to my mother. The big blond man. He's a Swedish psychologist, would you believe.'

'Nice looking man.'

'Certainly is. Those are the kind of men we like. Aren't they, Ollie?'

Sandra's husband had come across to join them, looking a lot more clean shaven than he often did. No, he explained to Mrs Sinclair, they weren't local; he was enjoying a few weeks gardening leave before he started a job with a different bank.

'And somewhere over there,' Sandra said, 'probably on the far side of the pond, is my elder sister Caroline. She's the other blonde one. With lots of children.'

'But, so far as we can see, no husband,' Oliver observed.

Mrs Sinclair chose not to comment. A waiter arrived to refill their glasses, and Sandra decided that it would be wise to go off and check up on what Toby was doing.

Meanwhile Edward, propelling himself around the garden with his stick, had encountered Paul Preece. Making sure that he wasn't speaking too loudly, as she was not too far away from them, he said: 'Dorothy's looking well. I think that new hair style suits her.'

'I agree with you. Harriet decided it was time her mother had a new look.'

'Makes her look younger.'

'Yes. I still find it a bit of a surprise seeing her with short hair after all these years, but you're right. And she's much happier now that she can see Harriet and the grandchildren more frequently.'

'And you have a son as well, if I remember correctly?'

'Ah, yes,' Paul replied, with a sigh. 'The long lost son.'

'He's been abroad?'

'He might as well have been, for all we've seen of him.'

Could it be, Edward wondered, that he's about to admit to screwing things up? This could be worth waiting for.

'Yes,' Paul continued. 'Something went wrong there, for some reason. And I have to agree with what Dorothy says about it. In our day we were expected to defer to our parents, and God help us if we didn't. Now it's even worse if we don't defer to our children. Dorothy's found it all very distressing.'

'And haven't you?' Edward enquired, more sharply.

'I haven't welcomed the situation,' Paul said, in his normal dry manner. 'But enough of that. Your garden's looking tremendous.'

'Best time of year for gardens.'

'You presumably have help with it?'

'Yes, we have proper gardeners now. Costs more than we used to pay to that stupid oaf Byron, but it's worth it.'

'The one who assaulted your daughter? That was a dreadful business.'

'It was. She still has nightmares about it. But Laura was brilliant with her. She does trauma recovery stuff, you know. It's brought them much closer together, too.'

'So three cheers for the social housing development. That's where he lived, wasn't it?'

'Yes, but to be fair, it could have happened anyway. He used to live down at the bottom end of the village.'

'Do we know what's become of him?'

'Not exactly. He's certainly not living here any longer. I think his mother was wanting to get him into the army. But that didn't work out.'

'You wonder what sort of job he could hold down, don't you?'

'A bouncer, possibly? He's certainly big enough. Anyway, Edith says his mother's a lot happier with things now she hasn't got him hanging around any longer.'

Edward moved away, noticing that – not for the first time – Mike Tayfield was busy talking to Caroline and helping her to keep an eye on her children. Edith had told him that Mike had separated from his wife; all quite amicable, apparently. He didn't want to go to London to teach, she felt she needed to because she worked in the fashion world, and they hadn't had any children. And Edward had deliberately broken his normal rule about not telling his adult daughters what to do with their lives. When Caroline's husband had finally got himself another job in the Midlands he had sat her down and advised her very strongly not to do what he wanted by following him there – and not just because of the disruption to their children's schooling and the slow down in the property market. Caroline, always the obedient wife, was initially reluctant to listen to him. However, Edward thought to himself, nodding in their direction as he continued his circuit round the garden, the more she sees of Mike the better. He's worth ten of Roger any day of the week, as well as being much better looking.

Once Edith had made sure that she had greeted all their guests she made her way towards Barbara.

'It's a while since I've seen Charles,' she said. 'He really has lost weight, hasn't he?'

'And he's being very good and sticking to the soft drinks,' Barbara replied.

'Good for him. Might do no harm for Edward to do likewise. He's starting to puff a bit by the time he's walked to the top of the garden.'

'Well, Charles didn't have a great deal of option. I think the hospital put the frighteners on him after he had that mini stroke just after Christmas. He hasn't had an attack of gout this year, either.'

'And exercising the new dog keeps him fit, too, I would imagine.'

'Oh, he regards that as fun.'

'Another Labrador?'

'Neither of us would have anything else.'

'Terrible, isn't it – I've forgotten the name of your previous dog already.'

Barbara chuckled.

'Officially he was called Becket. But he ate so much I'm afraid we all took to calling him Bucket. We're trying not to over-feed this one.'

'And you've put Charles on a diet, too?'

'Sort of. He still gets plenty of food, because he needs it. But the once a week treats have gone back to once a month.'

'And he's not getting bad tempered about it?'

'He's being remarkably good about it. Mind you, the other day we drove past a pub called the Cock and Bottle and he said rather mournfully that the only time he has any fun with either these days is when he has to go to the surgery and do a pee for the nurses.'

'Poor old Charles. Still, we're all getting older.'

'I'll say this for Charles; when he commits to doing something, he's very diligent about sticking to it. He's always been like that. I suppose it's one of the disciplines he learned from being in the Army.'

'He certainly stuck to his campaign about the housing development.'

'Well, he had that nasty little man Thomas prompting him the whole time,' Barbara said, sounding aggrieved.

'Yes, I can't say I'm sorry he's moved away. Has anyone any idea where they've gone?'

'Some ground floor flat near the coast. It'll be much better for her.'

'She certainly made her point dramatically enough last summer. So is Charles reconciled to what's happened at Church Field?'

'Oh, he still chunters on about it. Between you and me, I think he keeps on about it so as not to lose face. It really doesn't make the slightest difference to us up here, does it?'

'And we haven't got Betty Henshaw banging on about it either. Do you know the latest about her?'

'Not in good shape at all. Waiting for some test results, I believe.'

Edith shook her head and said: 'Well, there's only so much of a hammering anybody's liver can take. She certainly tested hers to destruction. We did invite her, but I don't think we ever got a reply.'

'That accident outside the shop really did for her. Lost her licence, though from what I gathered she wasn't in any way to blame for what happened. Then retreated home with a bottle and she's hardly been seen since.'

'Has anyone been trying to help her?'

'I understand Dorothy Preece called on her, you know what a kind soul she is. But it was rather like trying to cuddle a skunk. Betty told her to go away because she was perfectly capable of ordering what she needed on line, and she'd never had much use for tea or for sympathy anyway.'

Dorothy and Paul came across to join them, and the conversation changed direction.

'Frank's just told us that the Housing Association's been taken over by a larger group,' Dorothy said.

'It's happening a lot,' Paul commented.

'Is that a good thing?'

'Could be. It never struck me as a particularly well managed outfit. Chief Executive retiring early on health grounds, and all that. That's usually a euphemism for somebody deciding that he wasn't up to the job.'

'But it won't make any difference to what goes on here, will it?'

'It won't change the tenancies, if that's what you mean,' Paul explained. 'But the Association it's joined has most of its housing stock further north. They may decide that Horton Fence is a bit out of their area, and sell Church Field to a different Association.'

'What?' Charles exclaimed, having heard what was said and adding himself to the group. 'You mean after all we've been through they're going to cop out and hand the thing over to someone else? Monstrous!'

'Calm down, Charles,' Barbara told him. 'Nobody's saying that's going to happen.'

Charles grunted and, seeing the waiter, asked for his glass to be refilled. 'And you can put a small amount of bubbly in with it this time, if you would.'

The waiter smiled. Barbara frowned. Charles decided it might be safer to continue a conversation with the waiter, and said: 'Tastes better, and might prevent me going indoors so often. The way things have been going recently I reckon I've a strong chance of being selected to piss for England.'

The waiter, who was Lithuanian and whose English wasn't up to this kind of social chat, smiled again and moved on to another group of people. Then a small boy rushed up and grabbed hold of Edith, saying: 'Grandma, Toby's thrown Helen's toy into the pond and I don't know where Mummy is.'

'All right, Richard,' Edith said. 'Let's go and find her.'

They set off together. When they were out of earshot Charles said: 'Probably gone behind a bush for a quick snog with Mr Tayfield.'

'Charles, behave yourself,' Barbara said. Then, turning to the Preeces, she went on: 'I'm beginning to be reminded of the comment Harold Wilson once made about Tony Benn. He said he immatured with age.'

'Nonsense,' Charles retorted, chortling. 'I've come to a good party on a lovely day to enjoy myself, and that's exactly what I'm doing.'

Paul and Dorothy went across to a table to park their empty glasses, deciding that the time had come for them to make an exit. As they went in search of Edward and Edith Dorothy said: 'I've just been talking to the couple who moved into the house where the doctor and his family used to live. Looks like I've got myself another church cleaner.'

'Hm,' Paul commented. 'Now that we're both about to become A Certain Age I think the time's come for you to give that up. You've been doing it for years.'

'Oh, no, I don't think I could do that. And anyway, Mrs Grayson's at least the same age as us. She may even be a bit older.'

Paul raised his eyebrows, but said nothing in reply.

'Well, what was your verdict on that?'

Edward and Edith were relaxing with another glass of wine after their guests had left. One of the advantages of hiring waiters was that they tidied everything away – though Jonas clearly felt the need for some egalitarian behaviour by helping them. Mike Tayfield had taken Caroline and her children off somewhere for a treat; Toby, who had qualified for what his father had described as a bollocking, was sticking close to his mother and behaving in an uncharacteristically subdued manner.

'Good to see most of the usual suspects again,' Edith said. 'Nice to have a few new ones, too.'

'That Grayson bloke's heavy going,' Edward observed.

'Oh, have mercy, Edward. The man was a quantity surveyor.'

'Ah. That explains a lot.'

'Though one or two have fallen by the wayside since we last had a do like this.'

'It happens. Most of us would be officially classed as elderly. There are a few who fall into the category called old.'

'Speak for yourself.'

'I wasn't doing. Personally, I prefer the label 'late middle age.'

Edith chuckled.

'I'm trying to remember when our last party was,' Edward said.

'Three years ago, I'd say.'

'You reckon?'

'Yes it was, I'm sure. That was when we were first starting to hear about the housing development.'

'And they were still going on about it today, some of them.'

'You wonder why they bother, don't you. It's a fact of life.'

'If not an entirely welcome one. Still, you know what I think, and my views haven't changed. But I keep them to myself. Now that Caroline's taken up with Mike Tayfield I'd have two daughters ranged against me.'

'And this is still a lovely place to live, isn't it? Especially on a day as good as this.'

'You're right. Spain's off the agenda. Just so long as you'll allow me to escape to the sun for a while when the winter gets unbearable.'

'It's a deal,' Edith said, stretching her hand out to him.

They were silent for a few minutes, and then Edith noticed that Edward was smiling to himself.

'OK. What's amusing you?'

'Oh, nothing much, really. Then, knowing that she would get irritated with him if he refused to answer, Edward said: 'I was just thinking about it being three years since we had our last party, and what my mother's typist would have made of it.'

'Eh?'

'Another thirty-six mouths have passed.'

An excerpt from

Internal Memorandum

J.C. Sledge

We spend a great deal of our time and our mental energy at work, yet the subject is hardly ever addressed in fiction. There are hopes, achievements and frustrations at work at work, just as there are in our personal lives. Similarly, there is humour, there are important relationships, and sometimes there are betrayals. What goes on in one aspect of our lives is bound to have an influence on what happens in the other.

As Martin Brown finds out…

Available price £7.99 from Brimstone Press
sales@brimstonepress.co.uk

Rachel arrived home for Easter full of bounce, blonde curls, and a small stud in the side of her nose. Martin thought it looked dreadful, but he managed not to tell her so. It took her all of three minutes to deal with the issue of her father's redundancy:

'Now that you've got the shove as well,' she told him, 'that makes four out of seven fathers in my group of close friends. If you're not back in work by September you should be able to get a much bigger grant for me next year.'

Next day she went out and got a job in a local pub. 'There,' she said. 'That's how to deal with cash shortages.'

At least she shows no signs of blaming me, Martin thought, and she's got more sense than to make noises about taking pity on me.

Adrian, by contrast, made no comment at all. He had become more settled since his escapades during his first term, and even got the occasional call from the friend they had taken away for the weekend in February. But neither Marian nor Martin knew whether he was feeling happy or whether he had merely found a way of keeping his discontents to himself. Perhaps I *should* have taken him to the pub after we'd done the directory round, Martin thought. He was making me an offer, and I pushed him away.

Martin's mother was less easy to deal with. She refused to accept that she needed a hearing aid, so telephone calls with her had become confused shouting matches which they tried to avoid as much as they could.

'You'll have to let her know when you ring to wish her a Happy Easter,' Marian said. 'We don't want another of her bouts of complaining that her family doesn't tell her what's going on.'

So, when Martin had fortified himself with another large whisky, he called her and included the news that he was looking for another job.

'Another dog? How long is it since your last one got run over?'

'Another *job*, Mother, not another dog.'

'What's the matter with your present one?'

'I haven't got one.'

'Why not?'

'There's a recession on, you know.'

'A procession, did you say? What procession?'

'I said a RECESSION, Mother.'

'What about it?'

'That's why I'm looking for another job.'

Pause. Martin was about to say Happy Easter, must go, when she went on:

'You mean you've got the sack?'

'Yes.'

'Speak up, I can't hear very well, you know.'

'YES.'

'Why? What did you do wrong?'

'Nothing.'

'Are you sure, Martin?'

'All right, everything, if that makes you feel better.'

'Pardon?'

'Never mind.'

'I can't understand what's wrong with the world these days. First Susan writes to tell me that her husband's up to his neck in debt because of some disastrous property deal, now you tell me you're out on the street. I've told her I'm not in a position to help her, so the same goes for you.'

As if you ever helped me, Martin thought sourly as he replaced the receiver and headed for the whisky bottle again.

With Marian's parents, who were told the news at a much earlier stage, there was simply a tacit understanding all round that the subject was not to be mentioned in Martin's hearing. And I don't want to be told what they say about it when I'm not there, Martin thought. I've always known they thought I wasn't good enough for her. They may both be ill and wobbly these days, but I'm sure they've got enough energy left for a good gloat. After all, my father-in-law's always right, I distinctly remember him telling me so.